A CALL TO CHARMS

A CALL TO CHARMS

A Forever Charmed Mystery

Denise Swanson

http://www.DeniseSwanson.com

A Call to Charms

ISBN-13: 978-0-9861017-6-2

A Call to Charms

From *New York Times* best-selling author Denise Swanson.

Chocolate, men, and magic.
Who can turn down that inheritance?

* * *

If life had gone as she planned, Lexie Green would have been teaching English at a prestigious university, not persuading spoiled, rich women to buy overpriced clothes they didn't need and often looked ridiculous wearing. Can you say electric yellow see-through skirts and Torn jeans with unfinished hems?

Still, although this isn't the life Lexie would have chosen, all is going well. At least until Lexie is fired and her deranged ex-boyfriend tries to kidnap her.

Deciding that it's better to accept a mysterious inheritance from a great aunt she's never heard of rather than end up kept in a cage as her ex's pet poodle, Lexie packs up and heads to Kansas. So, what if she has to go by a new name and live in a town that she can't find on a map?

Unfortunately, once she arrives in her new hometown, everyone there seems just a tad off-kilter and Lexie's cousin insists that the citizens are magical. At least there are a couple of hot guys hanging around for eye candy.

Even though Lexie doesn't believe the nonsense about her being the Ravenscraft Shield, she does believe her father was murdered—a father she never knew existed, and she investigates his death.

Too bad whoever killed her father now wants Lexie dead as well.

* * *

Series description:

First in Denise Swanson's new Forever Charmed paranormal mystery series.

For more information, please visit www.DeniseSwanson.com

CHAPTER ONE
As Fate Would Have It

Some people think what I do is magic. Others think it's a trick. Who's right? Truth be told, I'm not sure anymore.

In my old life, when I was Lexie Green, I used to laugh at my boss for believing I had special powers, but in my new hometown, where I'm Alexandria Ravenscraft, I don't find it quite so funny. Maybe it's because of how I got here, or maybe it's because in Echo Springs, Kansas the idea of magic doesn't seem as far-fetched as it did in Chicago, Illinois.

In hindsight, I wasn't exactly a stranger to the bizarre. There had been several odd occurrences in my past I'd brushed off as flukes. I should probably have recognized those incidents as early warning signals for the freaky events of the last week... but I didn't.

Which was why, when an aunt I had never heard of died and left me her store, I was totally unprepared for what was about to happen. Even when my newfound cousin and my aunt's attorney tried to fill me in as to the business's true nature, I'd thought they were crazy and refused to believe them. I'd like to say dismissing their advice was my only mistake, but I'd be lying.

It all started last Thursday morning fifteen minutes into my shift at Crystal's Closet. Working at an upscale clothing store, even a shop on Chicago's Magnificent Mile, had not been one of my life's goals.

It was a job I had taken purely to satisfy my creditors... and maybe a tiny bit to feed my craving for designer clothing at employee discount prices. But then a funny thing happened. I

1

became famous—at least among the city's chichi boutique owners.

Yes, that's right. I was the top salesperson—oh, excuse me, I mean fashion consultant—in the business. When I waited on someone, she didn't leave the store without putting a significant dent in her Sugar Daddy's American Express. Thank goodness, that kind of woman never leaves home without it.

This type of recognition wasn't the kind I'd always hoped to achieve. And I certainly never thought I'd be best known for parting vacuous women from their cash. But, hey, fate had dealt me a bad hand, and you couldn't blame me for using whatever cards I had up my sleeve.

My ace of spades was a knack for sensing people's innermost emotions, which allowed me to sell nearly anything to the trophy wives and spoiled daughters of the city's wealthiest families. Even the monstrosities the fashionistas inevitably come up with to see if we're paying attention flew out the door if I needed to get them off the rack to earn my bonus.

Electric yellow nearly see-through skirts: check. Torn jeans with unfinished hems for five hundred dollars a pair: absolutely. Drop crotch pants: sure. Who doesn't want to look like you're wearing a loaded diaper?

No. I don't put a spell on these women or read their minds. What happens is that I'm able to step into their Jimmy Choos and detect both their needs and insecurities. Back then, if I'd had to guess, I would have said I did it by observation and intuition. But frankly, I never looked too closely at the how or the why and just concentrated on the end result.

All I was sure of is that I had to concentrate extremely hard and really want to know how they're feeling. It's not as if I casually tapped into everyone I pass on the streets. Which was definitely a good thing.

I will confess that if I had a particularly demanding day at the store, occasionally I connected by accident. It's as if I'd forgotten to turn myself off and zeroed in on anyone experiencing a strong emotion.

Generally, it wasn't a problem, unless it happened with people who were close to me, which is why I was mostly a loner. And my one attempt to have an intimate relationship taught me that a boyfriend was out of the question.

Gil Osborn, the man I'd tried dating, just hated it when I tuned into him. He claimed it was weird. Although, I don't know why he cared because he always denied that I'd read his feelings correctly, anyway.

He was an attorney with a prestigious Chicago law firm, and considering I have a couple of college degrees I'm not using, at first, I found his ambition and drive a turn on. His OCD tendencies simply added to his initial appeal.

Anyway, that's what I told myself, so I didn't have to admit the idea of his ginormous salary and massive future earning potential weren't the real reasons I was going out with him.

Don't judge! Just because I mentally made fun of my customers didn't mean that I didn't want to be them. Or at least have their money. Prada suits, Ferragamo shoes, and Gucci purses don't grow on trees, at least not the elms lining Michigan Avenue. And Chicago is an expensive city to call home.

Still, my conscience nagged me until I ended up admitting to myself that Gil was not my Knight in Custom-Tailored Armani, and it was time to stop seeing him. To my surprise, he didn't take the breakup at all well.

Who knew he was that into me? He sure never showed it. If I'd any idea he'd be so upset, I'd have handled the situation differently. Say a message in a bottle thrown into the ocean from a beach in Hawaii.

However, it had been a month since his last pleading, cajoling, somewhat creepy text, and I thought he was a problem I could mark solved. Not that there weren't plenty of others waiting to take his place. Problems that is, not boyfriends.

In fact, if the look on the face of the woman who had just marched into the shop's door was any indication, I was about to add a new problem to my list before I even had my first coffee break. Although Ms. Ticked-Off wasn't one of my regulars, she looked somewhat familiar, but the motes of anger floating around her like fluff from a cheap feather boa made it hard to come up with a name.

Thankful that I was already serving someone, I quickly averted my gaze and focused on my current client. He was trying to pick out a birthday present for his wife or niece or secretary. I wasn't entirely clear who the gift's recipient was since his story kept changing, and truthfully, I really didn't give a hoot. As long as it had a four-figure price tag, he could give it to his pet monkey for all I cared.

As I held up various Hermès scarves, Vuitton belts, and Alexander Wang handbags for Mr. Evasive's inspection, I could feel Ms. Ticked-Off's glare burning a hole between my shoulder blades. And when out of the corner of my eye, I saw her wave away the three other consultants who approached her, I knew I was in trouble.

I wasn't at all surprised that as soon as I had rung up my customer's purchases and walked him to the door, Ms. T-O stomped towards me. She was still moving forward when she thrust a silver and black garment bag at my chest. She had the handle of the hanger aimed at my heart, and to save my brand new, silk, Roberto Cavalli blouse from being torn, I snatched the bag out of her hands and hung it on a rack near the closest register.

Once she was disarmed, I said, "May I help you, madam?" I thought the "madam" was a bit much, but my employer, Crystal Van Dyne, insisted, and you never knew if she was watching you on one of the spy cams she had hidden around the store.

"Yes. You can take this back and give me a refund."

I peeled the plastic off of a tomato red Valentino evening gown. As I examined it, I watched its owner fidget—smoothing the sides of her ash blonde chignon, tugging at the skirt of her Chanel suit, and toying with her Harry Winston pink diamond ring.

Why was Ms. Ticked-Off suddenly so nervous? Crystal's Closet had a liberal return policy. The only stipulation was that the customer had not removed the security tickets attached to the garments, which was to ensure they weren't worn before being returned.

Duh! That was it! She was trying to scam us. She had worn the dress, and either taken off the tag or it had come off when she tried to tuck it out of sight. Now that I had figured out her scheme, I could see a trace of deodorant under the gown's sleeves and faint wrinkles across the lap.

When Ms. Ticked-Off first appeared, I hadn't wanted, or for that matter needed, to tap into the woman's feeling. It was abundantly clear she was in a bad mood. But now I concentrated, and I could see there were guilt and confusion mingled with her fury.

Furthermore, for some reason, she resented me. *Where was that coming from?*

In a way, I was sorry for her, and the women like her, who spend thousands on a gown they can only wear once or twice. But not sorry enough to face the wrath of Crystal and take the dress back.

Trying to keep any hint of accusation out of my voice, I said, "I'm sorry, madam, the tag seems to be missing."

"Then put on another one and credit my charge card." She flung the receipt on the counter.

A quick peek at it told me her name was Caryn Underhill—

I didn't want to slip up and call her Ms. Ticked-Off to her face. "I'm so sorry, Ms. Underhill, but the store policy doesn't allow me to take back garments when their tags have been removed."

Eyes shiny with tears, the woman shrieked, "You young beautiful girls think you can get away with anything, but you can't. You'd better take it back, or I'll blackball this shop."

For an instant, I was distracted with her description of me. I'm neither young nor beautiful. My thirtieth birthday was already rearing its ugly head in the rearview mirror—and you know they say that those reflections are much closer than they appear.

Also, I'm not beautiful. While I have long copper-colored curls and unusual variegated green eyes, my generous curves were not what the magazines and movies tell us are attractive. Heck, half the designer lines the shop sold didn't have clothes in sizes large enough to fit me because most of the fashion world doesn't recognize any size beyond a ten, sometimes smaller.

"You forced me to buy this dress." Ms. Underhill's screech drew my attention back to her. "It's all your fault."

Despite both her complimentary assessment of my physical attributes and my good intentions to remain nonconfrontational, I blurted out, "How could I force you to buy anything? Did I wrestle you to the ground, steal your AmEx from your wallet, and sneak the dress into your car when you weren't looking?"

As soon as the words left my mouth, the English muffin I'd had for breakfast turned into a hockey puck in my stomach. Up until then, though I'd had a bad feeling about the situation, I had clung to the belief that I could dissuade the woman from full attack mode. Now that hope fizzled out like a used up sparkler.

Ms. Underhill's first reaction was shock, but she recovered quickly and screamed, "I don't know how you did it, but I've been talking to my friends, and they all say they end up buying more than they intend to when *you* help them."

6

Damn! "What in the world are you talking about?" I had been extremely careful not to nudge someone into purchasing a garment she didn't really want, but I hadn't taken into consideration the effect of buyer's remorse.

"You put some kind of spell on us."

Ms. Underhill's voice had reached the level of an emergency siren, and I knew Crystal would be flying out of her Batcave any minute now. Thank goodness, at the moment there were no other customers in the shop.

I took a step closer to her, intending to try to calm her down, but Ms. Underhill put her two index fingers together in the shape of a cross and held them toward me, squealing, "Stay away from me, you, you, sorceress."

There haven't been many times in my life I've been speechless, but this was one of them. How could I go from a successful fashion consultant to a wicked witch in less than a minute? Had there been a tornado I somehow missed?

I knew my mouth was hanging open and I should say something, but no words came to mind.

"See! See!" My inability to speak seemed to both infuriate Ms. Underhill and convince her she was correct in her assessment of me. "I'm right. You *are* putting some kind of hex on us."

"Are you nuts?" Her crazed expression got my tongue moving—that, and the fact I was afraid she was about to burn me at the stake. "Of course, I'm not a witch. If I had those kinds of powers, would I be wasting my time waiting on parasitical women like you?"

Oops! I shouldn't have added that last part.

Ms. Underhill's carefully microbladed eyebrows shot into her hairline, but before she could explode or accuse me of being Dracula or Tinker Bell or ET, Crystal glided up to us and asked, "Can I be of any help?"

Crystal had been a model and had maintained her slender figure, mane of thick blond hair, and beautiful complexion. I knew her body was due to extreme diet and exercise, and her smooth skin had Botox to thank, but I wasn't sure if her hair had any helpers or not. And I sure wasn't ever in the position to ask her.

Ms. Underhill's face now matched the gown she had been trying to return, and she pointed at me and screeched, "I demand you fire this, this demon right now. She forced me to buy a dress I didn't want, and she refuses to take it back. And," the irate woman finished triumphantly, "she was extremely rude to me."

"I beg your pardon, but that's not what happened." I was determined to make sure Crystal knew my side of the story. "For some reason, Mrs. Underhill thinks I have superpowers that compelled her to make a purchase she didn't intend to, but that's just ridiculous."

"Lots of us think that." Ms. Underhill stuck out her chin, which made her look like a sulky two-year-old.

"And I wouldn't take the garment back because she removed the tag."

Crystal narrowed her eyes, and I could see she was starting to take my part until Ms. Underhill played her trump card. "Furthermore, she called me a parasite."

"Well, she called me a witch."

Crystal turned her death-ray stare on me, and said, "I know you're both upset."

"Upset? I'm way past upset, possibly into stroke territory." The pulse beating wildly in my throat reminded me I wasn't exaggerating.

Crystal went on as if I hadn't spoken, "But, Miss Green, there is no excuse for being rude to one of our treasured clients."

She paused, and the three of us stood in a curious tableau. Sort of like the scene from *Gone with the Wind* when all the society ladies glower at Scarlett for daring to dance with Rhett while she was still officially in mourning.

Crystal's glare had been known to wither roses at two hundred paces, but I could see the tug-of-war going on in her mind. Who would triumph? Valued customer or ace salesclerk? Surely, I sold more than Ms. Underhill bought.

Just when it looked as if I would win, Ms. Underhill's voice cut through the silence like Zorro's sword carving a Z on his enemy's backside. "If you don't fire her immediately, not only will I tell all my friends to stop shopping here, I will mention how awful this store is when *Chicago* magazine interviews me tomorrow for their 'Stylish Chicagoans' article."

Oh, oh. The tide had turned, and now I was the only one left in the water with the circling shark and a big bull's-eye painted on my butt in blood.

Crystal took Ms. Underhill's arm and steered her to the register. "Here, let me credit your account for the dress, and you must pick out one of our lovely silk camisoles to make up for your trouble. We just got a new shipment from Sophie Simmons."

I was letting out a sigh of relief, thinking Crystal had distracted Ms. Underhill from continuing to demand my dismissal, when the harridan pointed at me, and said, "That will be fine, but I still want her fired."

"Very well." Crystal flicked me a dismissive glance. "Miss Green, your services are no longer required. Please gather your belongings and leave immediately."

Even that didn't appear to satisfy Ms. Underhill. She yelled after me as I headed to the back room, "And don't try to get a job at any other shop. I'm personally spreading the word to every boutique from here to New York."

CHAPTER TWO
It's a Bad, Bad, Bad, Bad World

It's strange, but I have no recollection of exiting the store. I'm equally mystified as to how I got home. The next thing I remember is sitting in my tiny apartment on the dilapidated sofa I'd been hoping to replace with my next commission check and gazing at the two neatly framed diplomas decorating the otherwise dull beige walls.

I had hung them with such pride. First my bachelor's degree, then my Master of Arts degree in English Literature. Years and years of hard work, I never put to any use.

Had I completed my Ph.D., I might have been able to join the faculty of a university, but without it, there was no way I could be a professor. I might be able to teach a few courses at a community college, but that would never be enough to make a living.

Why hadn't I studied something practical, like nursing or engineering? Could it be because I fainted at the sight of blood, and I was allergic to math?

Now it looked as if I couldn't even keep a position as a sales clerk. A job I would have sneered at back when I dumped my high school boyfriend because he would never be more than a stock boy at the local Meijer.

Karma was such a bitch. It had taken her a few years to prove it, but now I realized that she'd only been waiting for the right time to show me just how badly I'd underestimated her fondness for irony.

What had happened to me? When had I decided to settle for less than I was capable of achieving?

Most likely, it was about the time my mother got sick. Our relationship had never been a warm and fuzzy one, but I couldn't turn my back on her when she called and asked for help. I used the money from my student loans for her medical bills. Then instead of finishing my doctorate, I went to work to pay off those debts.

While I sat there, contemplating the ruins of my life, the sudden feeling of ants swarming up and down my legs made me leap off the couch. My foot connected with the wastebasket sitting next to the shredder—both positioned for easy access when I sorted the bills from the junk mail—and I swore as rubbish spilled across the worn tan carpet.

As quickly as it had materialized, the scurrying sensation disappeared, and I knelt to gather the crumpled papers, flattened Starbuck's cup, and used tissues. Scooping them up, I attempted to stuff the trash back into the container, but something was in the way.

I reached inside and drew out a large manila envelope that was wedged crossways a few inches below the basket's rim. As I touched it, a chill ran up my spine, and I quickly flung the envelope away.

The postal carrier had delivered it before Christmas, and it was almost Easter. Since then, I'd emptied my trash several times, at least once a week. How could I have missed it? It should have been long gone, already processed through some recycling plant and starting a new life as a copy of the Chicago Tribune or a Dunkin' Donuts napkin.

The reappearance of the packet reminded me that today's disaster was not the first shock I'd recently received. How could I have forgotten the little bolt from the blue staring at me from the floor?

Of course, I hadn't really forgotten it. I had deliberately repressed it, putting it in the section of my subconscious where I locked away all the other things I didn't want to think about. Repression and compartmentalization were talents I had honed to perfection during my unhappy childhood.

Now, as I sat cross-legged on the carpet, picked up the envelope, and slid my fingernail under the metal clasp, I hesitated. I was more than half-convinced I should get up, step over to the shredder, and get rid of it once and for all. Instinctively, I knew that opening this packet would set events in motion that were probably best kept from starting.

Then again, the fact that I was sitting on the floor unconcerned that my expensive skirt was in danger of being ruined probably meant that the apocalypse had already begun.

As I wavered, an electric-like tingling zipped up my arm, making me wonder if I was having a heart attack. Considering my day, I was entitled to at least a minor coronary. Before I could find my cell phone to call 911, the prickling stopped, and now it felt as if my hand was being nudged until I bent open the metal prongs and tipped the packet's contents out onto my lap.

The three envelopes—one long business-sized, one small, and one six-by-nine manila—seem to mock me, *Thought you could get rid of us, eh? Nice try, but no cigar.*

Previously, I had only read the business-sized letter. After scanning it the first time, I'd jammed everything back into the packet, told myself it was all a scam and threw it away.

Even then, in my gut, I somehow knew the letter was legit, but I just couldn't deal with what it said. This time when I slid out the single sheet of heavy white bond, I examined it more closely. The letterhead was that of a law firm in Echo Springs, Kansas

DEAR MS. GREEN:

I REGRET TO INFORM YOU YOUR GREAT-AUNT, PANDORA RAVENSCRAFT, DIED DECEMBER 14. AS HER ATTORNEY, SHE HAD PREVIOUSLY INSTRUCTED ME

THAT UPON HER DEATH, I WAS TO SEND YOU THE
ENCLOSED ITEMS AND TO INFORM YOU THAT YOU
ARE HER SOLE HEIR. CONTACT ME AT YOUR
EARLIEST CONVENIENCE TO SETTLE HER ESTATE. I'M
ENCLOSING MY CARD WITH BOTH MY OFFICE AND
CELL PHONE. PLEASE FEEL FREE TO CALL DAY OR
NIGHT.
 SINCERELY,
 WILLIAM MAYER

The same instant disbelief flashed through my mind now as
when I first read the letter. I had never heard of Pandora
Ravenscraft, and my mother had always insisted we had no
living relatives.

As recently as a month or so ago, during a rare telephone
conversation with my mom, I had mentioned the possibility of
trying to look up my roots. I had explained about a coupon I had
for one of those DNA ancestry companies, and she'd laughed,
and then told me not to waste my money. She'd insisted that we
didn't have any surviving family for me to find.

The slight waver in her voice told me she was not only
lying, she was afraid of something. But as I've already
mentioned, denial is one of my best talents, so I didn't press her
for the truth.

Reluctantly, I picked up the smaller envelope, which had a
strangely soothing scent I couldn't quite identify. I slit the flap,
and the notepaper inside glowed whitely. When I tried to look
away, it was as if my head was being held in a vise and I
cringed, as the dark purple ink appeared to hover above the page.

Bold handwriting commanded my attention:
DEAR NIECE,
IF THIS LETTER IS IN YOUR POSSESSION, TWO
EVENTS HAVE COME TO PASS. I HAVE DIED, AND YOU
ARE AT THE POINT IN YOUR LIFE WHEN YOU NEED TO

KNOW THE TRUTH ABOUT YOURSELF.

Before I could read further, I heard an odd scraping kind of noise. Because my entire apartment consists of a galley-style kitchen, a tiny living room, and an even smaller bedroom, I could survey most of it from where I sat.

While I was scanning the area, trying to locate the source of the sound, I heard it again, but this time I saw the front doorknob turn. There were more grating noises, then a thump as something solid hit the wood.

Shit! Someone was trying to break in, and I had forgotten to put on the deadbolt and chain. All that was standing between a burglar and me was a thumb lock any kid could open with his school ID card.

If Darwin was right about natural selection, I certainly wouldn't be surviving, because I clearly wasn't the sharpest cheddar in the deli case.

The door swung inward, and I rose to my feet, gripping the letter opener I had used to open my aunt's note. I was ready to defend myself to the death with a six-inch piece of metal whose plastic handle was stamped: SOUVENIR OF THE EMPIRE STATE BUILDING.

A man stepped inside, and I opened my mouth to scream, but before I could summon enough breath, I realized that the person standing in my tiny foyer with a startled look on his weaselly face was my ex-boyfriend, Gil.

We stared at each other for a long moment, then at the same time, we both said: "What are you doing here?"

Feeling silly, I slipped the letter opener into my skirt pocket and stated the obvious, "I live here." I couldn't believe he was in my apartment. I distinctly remembered getting the key back when we broke up. Had he forced the lock? "How about you?"

"Uh..." He ran a hand through his uncombed blond hair. "I was going to surprise you, take you to dinner when you got home." His chin was stubbled, and his face lined with fatigue. He'd always been a bit pudgy, but now his stomach overflowed his belt. It looked as if he'd been living on fast food and alcohol. "I miss you."

"Get over it." I'd had a bad day and wasn't in the mood to baby his ego.

"I can't. You've got to come back to me." Tears welled up in his bloodshot blue eyes. "I've tried, and I can't forget you."

"I'm sorry, Gil." I took a deep breath and tried to be gentle, but my patience was wearing thin. "We've been over this and over this, I just don't feel that way about you anymore."

"Then you leave me no choice." In a heartbeat, his expression went from lovesick to loathing. "The only way I'll ever get you out of my head is if you're dead." He pushed aside his suit jacket and drew a pistol from the waistband of his pants. "Since you won't come back to me, I'll have to kill you."

At first, I thought he was bluffing, but then I remembered the day I had found the gun he was now pointing at me. I had been snooping through his dresser, and there, underneath his tighty whities, was a Smith & Wesson. He caught me examining it, and when I asked why he had it, he told me shooting helped him relax.

At the time, I assumed he was referring to target practice, not gunning down ex-girlfriends.

While I had been strolling down memory lane, Gil had maneuvered himself, so he was behind me. Now he whispered in my ear, "If you're a good little pet, maybe I won't kill you. Maybe I'll just lock you up until you fall back in love with me."

"What?" I turned just in time to see him raise his arm. You really do see stars when someone hits you over the head, but they aren't the pretty sparkly ones or the dancing type, just pinpricks of bright light.

As I processed the pain, a piece of advice from a self-defense course that my mother had insisted I take the year I grew breasts popped into my mind. So instead of struggling to remain upright, I sprawled on the floor, pretending to be unconscious.

Gil nudged me with his toe, but I didn't move. Watching him from beneath my lashes, I saw him return the gun to his waistband and bend to lift me. When he couldn't, he settled for dragging me to the sofa and rolling me on to it. Then he left me there and walked back toward the door. I could hardly believe my luck.

I knew I only had a few seconds to make my move. There was no way I would be anyone's love slave...well, maybe Jason Momoa's, but only for a long weekend—ten days at the most.

Gil swore, and I saw he was trying to get a roll of duct tape started. While he was distracted, I snaked my arm out and reached for the wrought iron lamp on the end table. Once I had a grip on the base, I eased to my feet. The movement must have gotten Gil's attention because he looked up. When he saw I was standing, he came roaring towards me.

Realizing my only chance at survival was to hit a home run, I tried to channel Babe Ruth. As soon as Gil was in reach, I swung the heavy lamp, putting all my not-inconsiderable weight into the motion. I connected with his head and shoulders, and he lurched once, convulsed, and collapsed on the carpet.

Immediately, I ran for my purse, snatched my cell phone from the outside pocket, and dialed 911. But before they answered my call, I found myself flat on my chest, the breath knocked out of me, and Gil's muscular body pinning my legs to the dingy carpet.

Acting purely on instinct, I arched my back. Bucking like a rodeo bull coming out of the chute, I screamed for help. His torso lifted for a second, then he grabbed my hair and yanked. The pain was incredible, and for a second I thought I was done for, but while he was punishing me by using my curls to smash my face into the floor, again and again, I managed to get my hand free. I reached into my skirt pocket and grasped the letter opener.

Timing would be everything. My heart was booming in my ears like a jet breaking the sound barrier. This was my last chance to escape. I waited until he pulled my head aloft, and then instead of resisting, I shoved myself upward with all my strength, slamming my head into his nose. He toppled off of me, blood streaming down his chin, and I plunged the letter opener into his chest. He shrieked, clawed at it, and when he couldn't get it out started to crawl towards me.

There was no place to go. I had managed to get to my feet, but Gil had me backed up to the far wall. As I waited there trying to remember the words to the Act of Contrition so I could confess my sins and go to heaven, there was a loud pounding, and a querulous voice demanded we be quiet or he was calling the authorities.

Gil froze.

When the front door popped open, I figured that either the mechanism that kept it fastened to the jamb failed because Gil had forced the lock when he broke into my apartment or God had sent someone to save me.

Once I saw that my rescuer was Mr. Boswell, I was pretty sure it was the former. My neighbor was no angel. Although he *was* getting closer with every frail breath. Older than a vintage Fortuny gown, he stood in the doorway peering through Mr. Magoo glasses and leaning on his walker.

Thank goodness for cheap construction, paper-thin walls, and nosy neighbors.

Gil lurched to his feet and ran for the door, pushed Mr. Boswell out of his way, and as he staggered down the stairs, yelled, "This isn't over. I'll be back."

Time seemed to stand still, and I wondered briefly if anyone would notice that the man passing them on the sidewalk had a letter opener sticking out of his chest. Probably not. After all, this was the city, and the inhabitants had doubtlessly seen much worse.

Abruptly, Mr. Boswell muttered something about not wanting to get involved and shuffled away. The slamming of his door broke my trance. I hurried to my own door and closed it. This time I remembered to engage the deadbolt and secure the chain. Dashing back to where I'd dropped my cell phone, I grabbed it and sobbed out my story to the 911 operator.

As I waited for the police, I wondered where my great intuition had been. I sure hadn't seen that coming.

CHAPTER THREE
Betwixt and Between

Despite Mr. Boswell lying through his false teeth and claiming he hadn't seen or heard anything, the police believed my account of the incident. They assured me that once they had located Gil, they would arrest him for domestic violence.

I kept myself together while the officers escorted me to the station and took my statement, but after that, I lost it. I have a vague memory of a marathon session of sobbing and swearing, and then the next thing I knew, someone was telling me Gil was in custody.

He was claiming I attacked him, but the evidence was in my favor. I had been the one to call the police, not him. The responding officers had personally witnessed the damage to my door lock. And he hadn't sought treatment for either his broken nose or the stab wound.

The police informed me he had removed the letter opener, and they hadn't been able to find it, which was fine with me. It wasn't as if I wanted it back or anything.

Still, as I left the station house, the officers warned me that Gil would probably be freed after his bail hearing the next day. They suggested I get an Order of Protection.

Yeah, right. Like that would keep a delusional ex-boyfriend from killing me or keeping me in a cage like his pet hamster.

It was late afternoon when the police finally dropped me off at my apartment. Intellectually, I knew I needed to come up with a plan for what to do when Gil was released, but every time I tried my thoughts drifted off, and I relived the moment he pulled his gun on me.

At one point, I wandered into the bathroom and found

myself staring in the mirror. A tiny scratch under my right eye and a single, thin line of dried blood on my cheek were the only outward signs I had been beaten. Even though my head hurt like the hounds of hell had used it as a Frisbee and my face was as tender as if I had just had dermabrasion, it didn't appear that Gil had inflicted any permanent damage.

Oh. My. God. Permanent damage. Until then it hadn't completely sunk in that I could be dead. Gil could have killed me. Had wanted to kill me. Had tried to kill me. I owed my life to a cheap souvenir and a crabby old man.

My legs went numb, and I sank to the cold tile floor shivering. My mind's eye focused on Gil's malevolent expression as he banged my head on the worn carpet, and I sat for what seemed like hours sickened by the raw hate I had seen on his face. Flashes from the assault exploded like a string of firecrackers in my brain until I could barely breathe, let alone figure out what to do before he got out on bond and came after me again.

It took a long time before I could finally turn off the horror movie playing in my head. I sucked in a huge gasp of air and forced myself to think about my options.

I could move or get stronger locks on my door. But what if he followed me or forced his way in while I was coming or going? A pit-bull would take care of that problem. But what if he shot the poor dog? A gun. I definitely needed a gun. One bigger than his. He had the Dirty Harry kind, I would get the Terminator model.

I leapt to my feet and ran into the living room. I was ready to arm and defend myself when it dawned on me I had no idea where to buy a gun, and even if I figured out how to purchase one, I didn't know how to shoot. Besides, hadn't I read somewhere that nine out of ten times a gun was turned on its owner?

Okay, what was plan B? I looked around and the envelope lying on the coffee table caught my attention. Could that be my solution? Considering I had no job, —and probably couldn't get one in a three-hundred-mile radius—a homicidal ex, and nothing to tie me to Chicago, maybe it was.

Hmm. It sure seemed like a good idea, and it wasn't as if I had a lot of time to come up with something better. Gil would get out of jail tomorrow, and if I were still around, he'd either kill me or measure me for a dog collar. And my hair didn't look good in a poodle cut.

Once he was out on bail, he'd be free until the trial. Furthermore, there was no guarantee he'd be convicted. Mr. Boswell wouldn't testify, which meant it was my word against his. An unemployed sales clerk versus a well-respected, high-powered attorney.

I chewed my lip, and then nodded. It was the only solution. I would claim my inheritance and disappear into the wheat fields of Kansas. I hadn't gotten to finish reading my aunt's letter, but the attorney's message had been plain. I was her beneficiary. All I had to do was show up. I just hoped her estate would be enough to get me started in a new life.

It wasn't as if I had a job or a family or a life... Why should I turn down the chance at a fresh start? Even if I didn't know the aunt who had left me her estate, I'd be crazy to refuse any kind of inheritance, especially since I no longer had a way to make a living.

Yep, I'd throw a few things in a suitcase, hop in my car, and not look back. No, wait a minute. I couldn't leave right now. To begin with, I wasn't in good enough shape physically or mentally to start a long drive, and second, my scheme would work better if I tied up some loose ends before I left. For once in my life, I had to curb my impulsivity, think the situation through, and have a comprehensive plan. This was my only chance, and I had to do it right, or I was screwed.

I glanced at the clock and was shocked to see it was already eight o'clock. There wasn't any time to waste. I wanted to be on the road by six the next morning, well before there was any chance Gil would get out of jail.

What should I do first? Find a computer. My laptop had fried a few weeks ago, and I hadn't gotten around to replacing it yet, and my cell didn't have enough data left on the plan to surf the web.

Normally I would have gone to the library, —no matter what little town or big city my mother had moved us to, the library had always been my place of refuge—but I wasn't sure if it was open this late. And even if it was, it was too far. Time was at a premium and there was a neighborhood cybercafé only a couple of blocks away.

Having a strategy spurred me into action. I grabbed my purse, stuffed the packet from my aunt inside, and hurried out of my apartment. It was raining when I reached the street, and, of course, I didn't have an umbrella.

Oh well, my clothes were already ruined from being dragged across the floor. I had a moment of regret for my black patent leather Manolo Blahnik pumps as I splashed through the first puddle, but somehow the thought of my imminent death put wrecking my shoes into perspective.

I was thoroughly drenched by the time I entered the E's To You café, and the teenage girl behind the register glared at me as I dripped on her floor. Shooting her an apologetic look, I headed to the ladies' room. There I used their extra roll of toilet paper to dry myself, scraped my sopping wet hair into a ponytail,— wincing as the brush pressed against my tender scalp—and dry-swallowed three Advil from the supply I kept in my purse.

Now that I was presentable, I returned to the café. There were only two other people in the place—the clerk and a boy in a

Blackhawks jersey leaning against the counter flirting with her. Once I'd taken care of the formalities required to use a computer, the lovebirds and I ignored each other.

I settled into the molded plastic chair in front of the monitor and reached into my purse for the packet from my aunt's lawyer. When I opened my aunt's letter it was no longer iridescent, and the ink appeared ordinary and two-dimensional, but the bold handwriting remained the same as the first time I'd looked at it.

DEAR NIECE,

IF THIS LETTER IS IN YOUR POSSESSION, TWO EVENTS HAVE COME TO PASS. I HAVE DIED, AND YOU ARE AT THE POINT IN YOUR LIFE WHEN YOU HAVE A NEED TO KNOW THE TRUTH ABOUT YOURSELF. NO MATTER WHEN I DIE, YOU WILL NOT READ THIS LETTER UNTIL THE SECOND CONDITION IS MET. I WILL EXPLAIN WHAT I'M ALLOWED TO SHARE. THE REST YOU MUST DISCOVER ON YOUR OWN.

FIRST, YOUR REAL NAME IS ALEXANDRIA RAVENSCRAFT. I HAVE ENCLOSED YOUR ORIGINAL BIRTH CERTIFICATE. YOU WERE BORN IN ECHO SPRINGS, KANSAS ONE MINUTE AFTER MIDNIGHT ON NOVEMBER 1 TO NATHANIAL AND MIRANDA RAVENSCRAFT. YOUR FATHER WAS MURDERED THE NIGHT BEFORE, AND AS SOON AS SHE WAS STRONG ENOUGH YOUR MOTHER TOOK YOU AND RAN AWAY, CHANGING HER NAME TO MELANIE GREEN AND YOURS TO LEXIE GREEN.

UNBEKNOWNST TO HER OR YOU, I HAVE KEPT TRACK OF YOU BOTH—HOW I WAS ABLE TO DO THIS IS ONE OF THE THINGS I AM NOT PERMITTED TO CLARIFY. GIVEN YOU ARE READING THIS LETTER, IT IS TIME FOR YOU TO ASSUME YOUR TRUE IDENTITY AND PURPOSE IN LIFE, AND TO COME HOME. TO

ASSIST YOU IN THIS, I HAVE PROVIDED YOUR BIRTH CERTIFICATE, A SOCIAL SECURITY CARD, AND A LIFE INSURANCE POLICY IN YOUR REAL NAME.

DO NOT TELL YOUR MOTHER ABOUT THIS LETTER OR INFORM HER OF YOUR WHEREABOUTS. IT WOULD PUT BOTH OF YOU IN GRAVE DANGER. YOU MAY RELY UPON MY ATTORNEY, ALTHOUGH HE IS SOMEWHAT NAÏVE, AND TRUST YOUR COUSIN, ELISSA MORNINGSTAR. ALL OTHERS IN ECHO SPRINGS YOU MUST JUDGE FOR YOURSELF.

AS YOU HAVE ALWAYS KNOWN, YOU ARE A SPECIAL PERSON DESTINED TO HOLD MANY LIVES IN YOUR HANDS. I HAVE SENT YOU ONE ADDITIONAL ITEM. IT HAS GREAT POWER, BUT CAN ONLY BE USED ONCE AND ONLY FOR THE TRUE PURPOSE. FOLLOW YOUR INSTINCTS.

ALL MY LOVE,

AUNT PANDORA

After rereading the letter ten...or a hundred times, my mind began to accept its contents. My name was Alexandria Ravenscraft, not Lexie Green, I was born on November first (not the fifth), and most importantly, my father was Nathanial Ravenscraft, not Jack Green, a man I had been struggling to remember my entire life.

My mother had always told me my dad died in a car accident when I was three, and that he loved me very much. She claimed to have destroyed all the pictures of him when she was crazy with grief. Now I wondered if a man named Jack Green had ever even existed.

Mom had always practiced what I called flexible facts. I wasn't sure if she deliberately lied to me or if her reality was just so elastic she thought she was telling me the truth.

I had to fight the urge to whip out my cell phone, call my

mother, and demand some answers. But even if my aunt hadn't warned me not to share any information with her, I knew I couldn't tell her my location. She'd be the first person Gil contacted, and he'd have no trouble getting her to spill the beans. He could be incredibly charming, and she was susceptible to handsome, no-good men. Turns out, I was more like her than I had thought.

There was also the little matter that since Gil was a hotshot defense attorney, I had no doubt he'd be able to get a hold of my mother's phone records, as well as mine. I didn't want him hurting her because he thought she knew more than she did.

As Aunt Pandora instructed, it was better for her if she genuinely had no idea where I had gone. It wasn't as if she'd be worried if she didn't hear from me. We were far from close. Heck. I hadn't seen her in over three years.

Once things settled down, I'd buy a disposable cell and call her. But for now, I'd let sleeping mothers lie and maintain radio silence.

Having decided not to telephone Mom, I opened the six-by-nine manila envelope. As my aunt had promised, it contained a birth certificate, social security card, and a small life insurance policy—the kind you can get for babies. I also noted that Alexandria's, I mean my, address on the insurance policy was in Echo Springs. I guessed it was Pandora's house.

The last item in the envelope was a flint arrowhead attached to a rawhide string. I hesitated, then slid it over my head. When I slipped it under my blouse, it nestled between my breasts. I was surprised the sharp edge didn't prick me, but after a moment, I couldn't feel it and was able to ignore its presence.

The Advil must have kicked in about then because my head felt much better as I turned to the computer. Thank goodness for the Internet. It didn't take me long to access the Kansas DMV and find out that the birth certificate and insurance policy would be enough proof of my identity to get a driver's license in the name Alexandria Ravenscraft. How my aunt had known I would need to change my identity and disappear was the million-dollar question.

I also found maps to get me from Illinois to Kansas, but none of them showed a town by the name of Echo Springs. Googling Echo Springs didn't help either, there was no mention of the community anywhere online. I sat stunned for a moment. I was moving to a town so small it wasn't even on the map. A shudder ran down my spine at the image of me trading in my Chanel suit and Prada purse for overalls and a pitchfork.

Mentally I slapped myself. If I were going to survive this next phase of my life, I'd have to stop being so superficial and keep focused on the crucial issues. Like, say, staying alive.

Before I left the café, I asked the clerk if she knew where I could find the nearest pay phone. She had no idea, but for twenty bucks loaned me her cell, telling me I had exactly ten minutes. I moved out of her earshot and dialed my aunt's lawyer. Mr. Mayer answered the phone on the first ring and seemed to be expecting my call.

Although I was grateful that he didn't ask questions or attempt to chat, I found it strange that he acted as if he knew I'd be phoning him and what I'd have to say. Still, with everything else that had happened to me that day, I probably shouldn't have been rattled by his behavior.

Shaking my head and focusing on what was important, I asked how to get to Echo Springs. Mr. Mayer told me once I got to Kansas, I was to take Interstate 70 west to U.S. Route 283 south and turn west on State Route 4. From there I was to drive about thirty miles, and just before reaching a city called Buffer, turn right onto an unpaved road with no street sign. I would cross a bridge over the Ricochet River, and my new hometown was about ten miles past that.

When I inquired as to Echo Spring's population, he said it hovered at a little over ten thousand, which surprised me. Wouldn't you think a community of that size would be on the map?

Before I could ask any more questions, Mr. Mayer hung up, and I knew that ready or not, it was time to return to my apartment. If the police were mistaken, and Gil had already made bail, he could be waiting for me there. If that were the case, I had just wasted my last evening on Earth scouring maps of Kansas, when I could have been chowing down on Chicago's famous Carson's ribs or Oberweis ice cream.

My luck held, and I made it back to my apartment without encountering my rabid ex. Thank goodness that although Gil had broken the thumb lock, the deadbolt still worked. And as soon as I got inside, I turned the key and fastened the chain.

I also pushed the couch and a bookcase against the door for good measure, but I still couldn't make myself get into the shower. With scenes from *Psycho* flashing through my mind, I settled for a sponge bath. But even then, I didn't get entirely naked.

Afterward, I put on flannel pajamas and my heaviest bathrobe. Just when I started to warm up, another surge of chills set my teeth clattering. Clasping a mug of hot chocolate, I started making notes of what I would need to accomplish before leaving the next morning. I ended up with two lists. What I wanted to take with me and stuff that had to be stopped or destroyed.

With the last one in mind, I revved up my shredder. Into it went every scrap of paper in my apartment. Okay, not the roll of toilet paper, paper towels, or cash, but everything else except the contents of my aunt's packet.

I alternated shredding and using my cell to stop my mail, shut off all utilities, cancel my lease and pay my bills—which pretty much drained my checking account. I had no investments,

27

retirement funds, or CDs, just a small money market account I'd empty at an ATM on my way out of town.

With all the clerical business taken care of, I smashed my cellphone. I'd read enough mysteries to know how easily it could be traced.

Next, I moved on to the problem of what to take with me. Living in a furnished apartment and not being much of a cook, there were few household possessions to worry about, but my wardrobe was a different story.

There wouldn't be room in my Camaro for all of it. When I bought the car used for under five thousand dollars, I had thought I had gotten a real bargain. Now I wished I had gone for one of the minivans I used to make fun of as I sped past them.

I knew it was silly and petty, but I cried as I stood in my closet and saw all the clothes, shoes, and purses I would have to leave behind.

While I was growing up, my mother had done all our shopping in stores that sold clothes right alongside the produce and kitty litter. Even as a teen, I'd known I'd rather have one really nice outfit from an upscale shop than five cheap ones from Wal-Mart, but I could never convince her of that fact.

Working at Crystal's Closet, I got a deep discount, first choice when merchandise went on sale, and the wonderful feeling of never having to wear second-rate clothes again. Since I'm not pencil thin, dressing in well-made, fashionable clothes helps me to feel good about myself, which was why figuring out what to leave behind was such torture. I loved each garment, shoe, and handbag as if they were my children, but I knew I would have to choose.

Besides having limited car space, I had a bad feeling most of my wardrobe wouldn't be appropriate for my new hometown. I ended up with three suitcases, a garment bag, and a cosmetic case. I left all but one of my favorite cocktail dresses, guessing there wouldn't be too many fancy parties in my future. I also left most of my designer suits, to have more room for pants, jeans, sweaters, and tops.

But the most heart-wrenching possessions to abandon were the shoes. The high-heeled Ann Taylors, pointy-toed Donna Karans, and strappy Stuart Weitzmans seemed to scream out to me when I closed the closet door on them. The designer purses wept more quietly.

After I put my luggage by the door, I grabbed a pair of scissors and went into the bathroom. It took me a few minutes of rooting under the sink until I found the box of hair color I had purchased a couple of years ago. I had never gotten up the nerve to try it, but now I had no choice. I would see if blondes really had more fun, whether I wanted to or not.

An hour later, my hair was the color of honey and barely brushed the top of my shoulders. Although I had done the best I could with the cut, I could only hope Echo Springs had a good hair salon.

After I disposed of the contents of my shredder and the packaging from the hair dye down the trash chute in the hallway, I couldn't think of anything else that needed doing. Sighing, I opened the bottle of Dom Perignon I had been saving for a special celebration. The end of my old life seemed a worthy occasion.

Normally, if I downed a whole bottle of champagne, I would have passed out, but not tonight. Questions swirled through my mind. How did my aunt keep track of me? How did she know I would have to change my identity? What did she mean by her statement, I would hold many lives in my hands? When she talked about my need to know the truth about myself, did she mean because of Gil's attack? But how could she know that would happen? And if she wasn't referring to my ex, was someone else trying to harm me? And, perhaps the biggest mystery of all, who had murdered my father, and why?

CHAPTER FOUR
From Fear to Eternity

Buzz! Buzz! Buzz! Groggily I hit the snooze button without opening my eyes. My head was pounding, and it took several seconds for yesterday's events to surface from the depths in which my subconscious had tried to bury them. When I recalled what had happened, my lids flew open, and I winced when the sunlight pouring through my bedroom windows seared my retinas.

Wait a minute, what was the sun doing out at five a.m.? Why wasn't it still dark? Moving my head was agony—no doubt, a combination of yesterday's repeated encounter with the floor and having chugged an entire bottle of champagne—but I turned it enough to peer at the clock radio on my nightstand.

The digital display read seven-forty-five, my usual wake-up time. *Shit!* I must have forgotten to reset the alarm. So much for an early start.

I crept out of bed, downed a couple of Advil, and crawled into the shower, angry with myself for messing up once again. When had I turned into my mother—drinking too much, missing important deadlines, and bumbling through the days?

Forgoing makeup for the first time in ten years, I donned blue jeans, a sweatshirt, and my old Keds, then peered into the full-length mirror. Dressed like this, with my wet hair and bare face, I looked like a teenager. Too bad I felt like an octogenarian.

Still, I needed more of a disguise. While packing, I had run across an oversized trench coat that had been part of my Halloween costume last year. The coat, along with a floppy rain hat and pillows belted around my waist, made me resemble Buddha.

Briefly, I brooded over the perplexing question of why it is almost impossible to appear skinnier than you are, but looking fatter is a snap. Then I shrugged and got to work on the next phase of my escape plan.

Having experienced an unsettled life with my mother, I had learned early on the art of moving without leaving any trace behind. Of course there was one huge difference this time. Mom and I were usually one step ahead of the bill collectors, not fleeing a homicidal maniac.

The first step of successfully vanishing is to make sure no one sees you taking off. So, after ascertaining that the hallway and elevator were empty, I began the process of transferring luggage to my car.

It took me three trips, and once I had all the suitcases in my Camaro, I returned to the apartment one more time to make sure I hadn't missed anything. My landline was ringing as I opened the door, evidently, the e-mail canceling my phone service hadn't taken effect yet. My breath caught in my throat as the machine took the call. Was Gil already out of jail?

"Lexie? Are you there? Pick up." It was Crystal. "Okay, I know you're angry about yesterday, but I've been thinking. How about you take a couple of weeks off with pay, then once things cool off you come back to work?" She paused, then said, "Call me today, and we'll make the arrangements."

What? I still had a job? Maybe I should stay. I thought about it for a minute. No, even if Gil wasn't threatening to put me in a cage like a prized parakeet, it was time to move on. To see where my real destiny lay. I'd read somewhere that no matter how hard you try, you can't stay even. It might feel safer that way, but unless you keep moving forward, you'll always fall behind.

Although I needed to burn rubber, I took a last look around my apartment. I had been there four years. Longer than I had lived anywhere before. Despite the fact that it was threadbare and tiny, it was harder to leave than I had expected.

Fighting tears, I tore myself away and got on the elevator. During the ride, I worried whether Gil might be waiting outside the garage exit. It was already past nine o'clock, and I had no idea when he would be able to make bail. If he was there, my only hope was he wouldn't recognize me in my off-season Santa disguise.

It was then that I realized my car was a problem. Although I rarely used it, Gil had seen the Camaro. I had no choice but to drive the car. If I sold it before I changed my ID and bought something new, Gil could find the records. And if I tried to sell it after I was Alexandria Ravenscraft, I couldn't prove that I was the legal owner.

Taking a bus or train to Kansas might work if there weren't cameras at all the stations. There was a good chance Gil would be able to get a look at the security footage and track me down if I bought a ticket.

I was at a stalemate. I had to drive my car, but maybe I could at least disguise the plates. Looking around for inspiration, I saw a small pile of mud near the right rear tire. A fistful smeared on both plates nicely obscured the numbers, and since my hands were already dirty, I coated my cheeks, too. I knew blackface was politically incorrect, but I was hoping for a pass due to the extenuating circumstance.

Glancing into the car's mirror, I rolled my eyes. Now, instead of Buddha, I looked like Fat Albert.

Hmm. Descending from a religious leader to a cartoon character in less than an hour—that was a record, even for me.

Having destroyed my cellphone, I didn't have access to a GPS, so I had to make my way to Kansas the old-fashioned way. Luckily I had an atlas in my car, another quirk I had gotten from my mother's lifestyle, and according to the map I-80 would take me to the middle of Iowa. After that, I'd get on I-35, which would allow me to cut through the northwest corner of Missouri.

My plan was to stop at Kansas City, Kansas and get my new driver's license, then find I-70 and follow Mr. Mayer's directions to Echo Springs. Too bad I didn't have the money to abandon the Camaro and buy a new car in KC. If I couldn't sell the Chevy, I couldn't afford a new vehicle.

I put the tote bag holding the packet from my aunt on the passenger side floor within easy reach. It would be the one thing I would only abandon upon imminent death.

Then after tuning the radio to AM 780 for the traffic report, I drove out of the garage. A few quick stops at various ATMs, and I was on my way.

Highway driving is hypnotic, and after several hours I had stopped checking my rearview mirror every two minutes, removed the pillows from around my waist, as well as the hat, and used a couple of Wet Ones from my purse to scrub most of the mud from my face. I would throw away the coat at my first pit stop.

My stomach growled, suggesting the pit stop had better be sooner rather than later. The only calories I'd had in the past twenty-four hours had been from a bottle of champagne, which reminded me, I also needed a bathroom.

Following a childhood of eating almost nothing but fast food, I had avoided that type of restaurant for the past four years. However, according to the information I had read online, the best way to disappear was to do the opposite of your usual habits. Therefore, I took the next exit and pulled into an Arby's.

Before going in, I stuffed the trench coat and hat into the Dumpster around back. I kept the pillows. No one had seen them, and they were expensive memory foam. I felt much better after a much-needed detour to the women's room where I washed off the remaining traces of the mud. My scalp was still tender when I brushed my hair, but my head wasn't pounding.

The menu had a bewildering array of options, and I finally surrendered and ordered by number, getting a beef and cheddar combo. Unfortunately, eating made me drowsy, but there was no time for a nap. Instead, I got a large coffee to go and prayed that I wouldn't fall asleep at the wheel.

I wanted to drive straight through without stopping at a hotel. The faster I got to Echo Springs, the less likely Gil would be able to find me.

Thankfully the caffeine helped, as did the great oldies station I found on the radio. Traffic was relatively light, at least compared to the Dan Ryan or Eisenhower, and if my homicidal ex was following me, he was keeping well behind.

Once, when I needed gas, I waited until the very last minute crossed from the extreme left lane to the exit, and pulled my car out of sight behind the station. Then I waited for the next fifteen minutes examining any vehicle and its occupants that drove in. There was no sign of Gil.

It was seven p.m. when I crossed into Kansas City, Kansas. So far, it had been a good day—no one had tried to kill me or capture me for his private petting zoo, but I did have one small problem. The Kansas City DVM was closed. I ground my teeth as I read the sign: HOURS 8:00 A.M.-5:00 P.M. SATURDAYS 8:00 A.M.-NOON.

If I had left at six in the morning like I should have, I could have avoided this dilemma. Now my only choices were to get a hotel and come back in the morning or to keep going and get a new license later.

It was tempting to drive on, but Echo Springs was another six or more hours away. I decided arriving at two in the morning wasn't the best way to slip into a small town without causing a lot of talk.

I tried to recall what moderately priced hotels I had noticed driving into Kansas City. I hadn't seen any on I-635, but about fifteen miles back, toward the airport, there'd been a bunch.

My only requirements were a clean room and parking in the rear. The Hampton Inn seemed to meet both criteria, with an added bonus of a desk clerk who was more interested in talking to her friend on her cell than noticing me. I registered as Jane Alcott in homage to two of my favorite authors, Jane Austen and Louisa May Alcott, and had my story ready in case the clerk asked for an ID or credit card. My purse had been stolen, and my cruel boss wouldn't let me miss this business trip.

But the girl didn't flicker an eyelash when I paid cash. She gave me my key, mumbled directions to my room, and went back to her phone conversation.

I was tired, hungry, and my head hurt. The enormity of what had happened in the past thirty-six hours had begun to hit me, along with a vision of what my future would hold. In short, I was crabby. Finding out the hotel lacked room service did not improve my mood, nor did the fact that the closest restaurant was a Cracker Barrel.

On the bright side, no one who knew me would ever think to look for me among the down-home rockers and giant checker games being played on top of wooden barrels.

After a gourmet meal of chicken-fried steak and mashed potatoes, I locked myself in my hotel room, changed into my pajamas, cleaned my face, and brushed my teeth. I had requested a ground-floor room and parked my car so that if I left the curtains open, I could see the Camaro out the window. Before climbing into bed, I checked to see if it was okay.

I was worried about leaving my luggage in the trunk, but I was afraid if I took it out, I'd never get it back in again. I had only brought in my nightgown, makeup case, and tomorrow's outfit. And, of course, my tote bag, which I would have Super Glued to my hand if at all practical.

It wasn't even nine-thirty, but I was exhausted, so I snuggled under the covers. I must have fallen immediately asleep because I woke with a start when bright lights flashed through my room. My first reaction was to hit the floor, then, as the lights moved on, I crawled to the window.

Making sure I couldn't be seen, I peeked over the sill and saw a hulking vehicle that almost looked like a tank backed into a space a few slots away from my car. It was too dark to tell who was inside.

A few minutes later, the SUV or truck or whatever the heck it was pulled out and came back toward my car. It slowed, then roared away. I crawled back to bed, trying to convince myself it was just some guy road tripping with a case of beer. The driver had probably been interested in my Camaro because it was a cool car, not because he was looking for me.

Surprisingly, I drifted back to sleep and didn't wake up again until the alarm went off at five-thirty. Given that I would have to get my picture taken for my new driver's license and also meeting my aunt's lawyer and possibly several other Echo Springians, I wanted to take the time to look nice.

Once I pried myself out of bed and started the tiny in-room coffeemaker, I hopped in the shower. As I sipped my first cup of liquid caffeine, I dried my hair and applied makeup.

After I donned black gabardine slacks, a white long-sleeved blouse with an oval rhinestone buckle on the self-belt, and Cole Haan black leather pumps, I ran to the lobby and grabbed a bagel and a glass of juice from the free buffet.

It was a few minutes after eight when I pulled into the Kansas City DMV parking lot, and although there were already people in line, my turn came quickly.

The process was going smoothly, my proof of identity papers had been accepted, I had passed the vision and written portion of the testing, and we had gotten into my car to take the driver's part when the examiners said, "Before we start, I need to see the proof of insurance."

My heart clenched and skipped a beat as I tried to figure out what to do. Had I shredded the insurance card with the rest of my papers? No. I kept it in the glove compartment with the registration, and I hadn't thought of them when I was in the midst of my destruction party. For once, a mistake was turning out to be to my advantage.

I smiled, reached across him, and retrieved the documents. "Here you go."

He studied them a long time, too long.

Shit! He would ask why the car was in someone else's name and I needed an answer.

He handed the papers back to me, and as I feared, asked, "Whose car is this?"

From his gray crew cut to his black oxford shoes, he looked like the working class guy on every TV show. Maybe if I claimed Lexie Green was my lesbian lover, he'd be too embarrassed to probe any further. No, that could backfire. What if he was a homophobe?

Okay, plan B, except I had no plan B and I could tell by the way he was tapping his pen on his clipboard he was getting impatient, so I blurted out, "Uh, my half-sister Lexie. We drove in from Chicago last night. She's helping me move to my new hometown."

I held my breath. Would he believe me or had I given him too much information and made him suspicious?

He nodded, made a note, and told me to start the car. By nine o'clock, I had my new license and was driving down I-70. I was a little surprised no one at the DMV had asked me why, at my age, I had never had a driver's license. I had prepared a story about growing up in the city and never needing to drive until I moved to Kansas to take a new job, but I hadn't needed to use that excuse.

Both the miles and the time were flying by and after a quick stop for lunch at a tiny country diner off State Route 4, I began to look for the unmarked street Mr. Mayer had described. When I got to the town of Buffer, I knew I had gone too far and doubled back.

Just as I thought I had missed the road again, I spotted it and made a sharp left. I could have sworn that the street had not been there the first time I drove past.

My life had always been a bumpy ride, but this was ridiculous. My poor Camaro was bouncing around like the marble in a roulette wheel, and I was fighting to keep the car steady when I felt a shoulder-dislocating jerk and knew I was in trouble.

I wrestled the Camaro to the side of the road, looped the straps of my tote bag across my chest, and climbed out. *Dammit! I had a flat.*

Swearing at it didn't make the tire re-inflate, so I dug the manual from the glove compartment. The instructions said the first thing I had to do was get the spare and the jack, which were under the floor mat in the trunk.

It had been difficult enough getting three suitcases, a garment bag, and makeup case into the car's tiny trunk. Getting them out was only marginally easier. When I spotted a huge black vehicle that I recognized as a Hummer burning up the miles, I froze and the luggage I was holding slid out of my hand onto the ground

The shiny surface of the Hummer seemed out of place on the gravel road, and as it got closer, the sight of my demented ex-boyfriend's face behind the SUV's windshield hit me like the blast from a nuclear bomb.

Shit! Clearly, he'd made bail a lot sooner than I'd expected, but how had he found me? Had he been following me the whole time? Snapping myself out of my terror-induced trance, I realized that it didn't matter how Gil managed to locate me because this wasn't the time to figure out his methods, it was the time to get the heck out of dodge.

Sprinting, I rounded the side of the Camaro and dove inside. Where were my keys? Had I left them in the trunk? No. I had shoved them in my pants pocket. I slammed the key into the slot, turned it, and mashed down the accelerator.

The car took off like a panther with an injured paw. I hung onto the steering wheel, using all my strength to keep the Chevy going straight. Unfortunately, the uneven road surface and the flat tire slowed me down. A lot.

Just as I started over an old wooden bridge, the Hummer caught up to me and rammed my rear bumper. As the Camaro skidded sideways, I looked down into the broad expanse of a fast-moving river. The water was flowing at quite a clip, whitecaps skipping along its surface and debris caught in the undercurrent.

The idle thought that western Kansas must have been having the same wet spring as Illinois flitted through my mind. It's amazing what pops into your head when you're busy trying not to die.

I somehow straightened the Chevy from the skid, but before I could drive away, the Hummer stopped, reversed, and came at me again. This time the SUV crashed into my Camaro harder, and I lost control of the wheel.

As the Chevy spun round and round, then smashed trunk first through the guardrail, my heart was making a valiant attempt to escape my body via my throat. At the last possible moment, the car stopped, its backend teetering above the river.

One more shove by the Hummer and the Camaro would plunge into the deep water below. The next few seconds seemed to tick by in slow motion as I tried to figure out a way to save myself.

Twisting my head to look behind me, I felt a sharp prick right above my left boob. Thinking a fragment from the windshield had fallen into my cleavage, I reached inside my blouse. But instead of finding a piece of glass, my fingers closed over the arrowhead necklace my aunt had sent me. I had forgotten that I had put it around my neck for safekeeping.

Intending to take it off before it drew blood, I grabbed the piece of flint and an odd tingling radiated from my palm all the way up my arm, to the center of my chest. Before I could analyze the sensation, a movement in front of me caught my eye, and I froze.

The Hummer was backing up again. Gil was lining up his SUV like a billiard stick, and my Camaro was the eight ball. As the massive vehicle rocketed toward me, the look of maniacal glee in my ex's eyes broke my stupor.

And despite being fully aware he couldn't hear me, I screamed, "May you burn in hell, Gil Osborn!"

Draping my purse strap across my body, I *wrenched* open the driver's door handle and threw myself out of the car. The instant my knees landed on the gravel surface, I got to my feet and *ran*.

A quick glance back revealed that Gil must have seen my escape from the Camaro. He was trying to turn his Hummer away from my car and towards me. But it was too late. Velocity and momentum kept the heavy SUV going forward. It smashed into the much lighter sports car and pushed it over the bridge's side.

Then, with a useless squeal of its tires, the Hummer followed the Camaro into the water. Transfixed, I watched as both vehicles rapidly sank out of sight.

I wondered how deep the river was. It had to be cold—winter had only officially ended a few days ago—and according to the mystery novels I devoured, once a vehicle is submerged it's nearly impossible to open the doors because of the water pressure.

Reluctantly I returned to the bridge. Not to save Gil—I wasn't one of those too-stupid-to-live heroines from some of the suspense thrillers I'd read. I walked back to make sure he was dead.

Surely, no one could have survived that plunge, but I needed to be certain he wouldn't come after me again. I was not spending the rest of my life in a cage next to his pet Pomeranian.

Nearly a quarter hour went by, and nothing and no one came to the surface. Turning my attention to my injuries, I saw that miraculously, I seemed to be okay.

Now that the adrenalin had subsided, I was starting to feel some aches and pains, and while both knees hurt, the discomfort wasn't any worse than when I had fallen off my bicycle as a kid. In contrast, my hands felt like they were on fire.

I winced as I picked out the pebbles and dirt from the abrasions on my left palm, then turned my attention to my right hand and blinked. Besides the scrapes from the gravel, it had a red and blistered triangular-shaped wound in the center of the palm.

After staring at it for a second, I realized it looked as if the arrowhead I had been clutching as I dove from my car burned its outline into my skin. Immediately, I reached for the piece of flint, but there was nothing around my neck except the leather thong. The arrowhead must have broken off the cord and fallen into the dirt when I jumped from the car.

Although I searched for the arrowhead for several minutes, it was nowhere to be seen. Also missing was one of the heels on my pumps. I tried to pry off the heel from the other shoe, but it wouldn't budge.

The footwear situation made me check out the rest of my

appearance. My beautiful black Armani slacks had split down the rear seam. Good thing I was too curvy to wear a thong. And my silky-white blouse hung in tatters from the collar.

Shit! Double shit! I had lost all my suitcases and would now have to arrive in Echo Springs looking like something that had refused to go down the garbage disposal. So much for blending in with the locals.

Sighing, I took a limping step toward my new hometown. An instant later, I stumbled to a stop. Before the Hummer had started to chase me, I had been about to change a flat tire. And that had required emptying the trunk to get to the spare.

My luggage hadn't gone to a watery grave with my Camaro, it was a mile or so back by the side of the road... unless someone got to it before I did.

I kicked off my ruined shoes and broke in a swift jog. Though I'm normally not a fast runner—the trainer at my health club despaired at the slow speed I selected on the treadmill—the incentive of reclaiming all my cherished clothing, shoes, and purses had me sprinting as if I was a chubbier version of Florence Griffith Joyner.

Flo-Jo had nothing on me as I spotted my abandoned luggage and raced toward the finish line. I sank down to the ground and gathered the precious bags into my arms.

While I sat on the ground, catching my breath, I realized my mad dash to rescue my belongings had been unnecessary. There hadn't been another vehicle on the road before or after the Hummer came after me.

Shoot! No cars meant I'd have to hike the last eleven miles to Echo Springs. How would I do that carrying three suitcases, a garment bag, and a makeup case?

When an answer didn't immediately pop into my mind, I pouted. I'd already left so much back in Chicago—my apartment, my job, my name, and my whole life. Impractical or not, I couldn't bear abandoning my prized wardrobe too.

CHAPTER FIVE
Wrong Day's Journey into Right

It took me a while to come up with a solution, but my luggage and I were finally making our way down the road when I heard a car approaching from the north.

At first, I was relieved at the prospect of a ride, but then I hesitated. After my recent experiences, and the warnings in my aunt's letter, how could I be sure that the occupant was a friend and not a foe?

After all, my ex, a man I could have sworn was Melvin Milquetoast, nearly killed me twice. My ability to judge human nature wasn't anywhere near as good as I had previously believed.

If I was smart, I'd hide. However, before flinging myself into the nearest ditch, I checked the time. It had taken me more than an hour to travel half a mile. I was pretty sure that the three suitcases I was dragging behind me like a trio of reluctant puppies were the reason I was so slow.

Although to be completely honest, it could also have been the garment bag and makeup case I was lugging in my other hand. Surely, the purse strapped across my chest wasn't the reason I was slower than a coffee pot brewing the morning's first cup of caffeinated heaven.

Then again, no matter what the cause for my snail-like progress, at the rate I was going, I wouldn't make it to Echo Springs until the Fourth of July.

Biting my lips, and with my stomach churning, I stood my ground while an elegant 1950s Bentley came into view. The shiny black car made a sweeping U-turn and purred to a stop in the middle of the road.

I was somewhat reassured when a short, rotund man of seventy or so hopped out of the car. His plush white hair, twinkling blue eyes, and pink nose reminded me of the rabbit in *Alice in Wonderland*. The notion was reinforced when he came toward me, peering at his pocket watch.

I half-expected him to mutter about being late for a very important date, but instead, he said, "Well, butter my butt, and call me a biscuit, look who's here." He snapped his watch closed, tucked it into his vest pocket, and grinned. "Miss Alexandria, you're the spitting image of Dora."

That had to be a nickname for Pandora, right?

Thinking that since my aunt's attorney was the only one who knew I was coming to Echo Springs it was reasonably safe to guess his identity, I said, "Mr. Mayer?"

"Call me Uncle Will." He took off his fedora, squashed it under his arm, and held out his hand.

"You're my uncle?" When we shook, I noticed his skin was soft, but his grip unexpectedly firm.

"I should have been, but Dora kept putting off the wedding. Then she died." He brushed at the jacket of his brown tweed suit.

"I'm sorry for your loss."

"Thank you. Yours too."

"Uh, right? Thanks," I stammered.

I wasn't quite sure if I had experienced a loss or not. Pandora might have been my aunt, but I hadn't known of her existence until two days ago when the devil's tornado had blown through my life sweeping my previous existence out the door.

Uncle Will took out his watch and looked at it again, then hurriedly started to load my luggage into his trunk. "We should get going."

After I helped him get my suitcases stowed away, I climbed into the passenger side of the expensive car. When Uncle Will took his seat, I had to hold back a giggle. He could barely see over the steering wheel.

Putting the Bentley in gear, Uncle Will drove off at a stately twenty miles per hour. At this speed, there was a good chance we still wouldn't make it to town until Independence Day.

Once I realized he wouldn't go any faster, I asked, "Where were you going before you rescued me?"

"To pick you up." He waved as he passed an old tractor hauling a farm cart.

"But..." I was bewildered. "How did you know I was here and needed a ride?"

Uncle Will ignored my question and pointed out a ranch on the right side of the road. "This land, for as far as you can see, belongs to the Furmans. They're one of the founding families of Echo Springs."

I spotted a sprawling farmhouse surrounded by a rail fence, set back on a piece of ground that was surrounded by acreage that still held the stubble of last year's crops. It was the first house I had seen since turning onto the unpaved road. "Why isn't that field planted like the one back there?"

"That was winter wheat, which is planted in September and usually harvested in June. They use this land for corn, which needs warmer weather. The next section is where the cattle graze." Uncle Will added, "The Furmans have owned this property since before Kansas became a state. The original settler married a Comanche chief's daughter."

Considering how little interest I had in agriculture or history, "oh," was the only thing I could think of to say. Besides, I needed answers to my questions, not a social studies lesson. "How *did* you know I was coming at this exact time?"

"That's not important." He was silent until we got into the city limits, then as we drove down Main Street, he nodded to a row of buildings consisting of a beautifully maintained old hotel, an elegant restaurant, and a 1940s style movie theatre. "These businesses all belong to Cole Pendergast."

"Impressive." The scene looked like one of those toy towns that department stores set up at Christmas time. Charming, but a little eerie in their perfection.

"The Pendergasts are also one of the founders of Echo Springs."

"How interesting," I murmured politely, then tried once again to get Uncle Will to answer some of my questions, "Speaking of interesting, a lot of peculiar things have been happening to me since I got your letter, and the coup de grâce was you showing up out of the blue precisely when I needed you. Just how did that happen?"

Uncle Will dismissed the question with a wave of his hand. "Right place, right time."

"Really?" Obviously, my dear "uncle" wasn't telling me everything.

He pulled the Bentley into a parking spot in front of an imposing red brick structure. Across the front window, WILLIAM MAYER, ESQ. ATTORNEY AT LAW was lettered in gold.

Uncle Will hopped out of the car and I followed suit, determined to make him explain what was going on. He held open the door to the building, and I walked by him into the reception area. To my left was a desk holding a computer and an overflowing inbox, and to my right was a sofa flanked by an end table stacked with magazines.

Silently, Uncle Will took my elbow and led me into his office. He indicated a pair of leather wingback chairs facing his desk, and I sat in the one nearest to the door. We seem to be at an impasse, and I tried to figure out his wants and needs as I did with the customers in the boutique, but couldn't get a clear picture.

Slightly alarmed at my inability to read him, I frowned. I

had never before been unable to read someone if I really tried.

While I was attempting to analyze my feelings about that, Uncle Will settled himself behind his desk, fussed with a stack of folders for a couple of minutes, then said, "As the firstborn of your generation, you've inherited the entire Ravenscraft estate."

"What does that encompass, exactly?" To me, the word estate meant wealth, but that wasn't the impression I had gotten from Aunt Pandora's letter.

He looked at the papers in front of him and reeled off, "The house and all its contents, the vehicle, all monetary assets after her debts have been paid, and, of course, Pandora's Candy Box."

The Candy Box part sounded good. Unlimited chocolates, caramels; oh, and the truffles, mustn't forget the truffles. But it didn't look like I'd be replacing my Camaro anytime soon. How much profit can there be from a candy store in a small town?

And, with my luck, the rest of my inheritance wouldn't be in the six-figure range either. On the bright side, if I owned a business, I wouldn't need to find a job, I'd already have one. I hoped my money held out until I could start working.

With my meager finances in mind, I asked, "How long until I can claim the estate?"

"Oh, that won't be a problem." Uncle Will peered at me over his half glasses. "I'm the executor, so you can move into the house tonight and start managing the store as soon as you're ready." He winked, and added, "And it looks as if you'll need Dora's vehicle right away too."

Now how could he know that? Why would he assume my car was permanently out of commission instead of broken down somewhere? I started to ask, but he shoved a pile of papers toward me and said, "Sign here, and here, and here."

"What are these?" I tried to read what he was asking me to sign, but the print seemed blurry when I attempted to focus. I shrugged it off, figuring that I was just too tired right now to deal with the legalese.

"Just documents I need to probate the estate for you."

"Uh, could I take them and read them tonight and get them back to you tomorrow?" I wasn't signing anything I hadn't read. My mother had had a lot of faults, but she hadn't raised any fools.

"Sure. Sure. No problem." Uncle Will gathered the papers up, swiveled toward a cabinet behind him, and then back forward, handing me a large manila envelope. "Didn't mean to rush you. I forgot you weren't raised around here and might not trust me as the others do."

What others did he mean? The Ravenscrafts? His clients? The whole town?

"Maybe I should get a hotel room until we get this all settled." I suggested reluctantly, mentally counting my limited cash.

"No." Uncle Will leapt to his feet, consternation written across his face. "Really. This is all a formality. The house and everything else is all yours. You're supposed to live there. It's the safest place."

"Safest place, what do you mean? Am I in danger?" Had I jumped from the frying pan into the fire?

"Uh, what I meant is, uh, safe as in comfortable. Your aunt wouldn't want you to stay in a hotel."

"Right." He was obviously holding something back, and just as plainly, he wouldn't tell me what it was, at least not today. "Then, if it isn't too much of an imposition, could you drop me off at the house? I'm pooped. I'd kill for a shower and some sleep." I was even too tired to eat. Hey, maybe I had finally found a diet that would work for me. What would I call it? *The Run for Your Life Weight Reduction Plan?*

"Now?" Uncle Will's little pink nose twitched. "But they're all waiting to meet you."

"All who?" My heart sank at the thought of meeting people. I'd changed into jeans and a sweatshirt after my clothes had been ruined in the accident, and I looked like I had been plowing the back forty or slopping the hogs. Not that I knew what either of those phrases meant.

"Well, they're a bit like the chamber of commerce." Uncle Will rushed on trying to entice me. "We're meeting at Cole's restaurant. There'll be lots of good food and wine. I'm sure you're hungry after your long trip."

"Why do they want to meet me?" I thought of what my aunt had written about being careful whom I trusted, but she had said I could rely on Uncle Will. "Were they all friends of Aunt Pandora?"

"Allies, associates, adversaries." Uncle Will tried to steer me toward the door, but rabbits don't have much in the way of herding abilities, and Uncle Will was more bunny than Border collie.

"Couldn't I meet them tomorrow after I've had a chance to get myself together?" I clutched my tote bag and refused to move. "If I met a few at a time, I'd have a better chance of remembering their names and stuff."

"That wouldn't be a good idea." The white mustache on Uncle Will's upper lip drooped. "It's important you be introduced to them right away, as a group, and with me to guide you."

What the...? He made it sound like I was the new queen being presented to the nobility for the first time. And they would decide whether to crown me or send me to the guillotine.

I was ready to give in, since this seemed so important to him, then I had an idea. "I'll make a deal with you. You answer my questions, and I'll go meet the aristocracy."

"What questions?" Uncle Will's bushy eyebrows met in a vee above his nose.

"The ones you've been avoiding since you picked me up."
My patience was growing thin.

He whipped out his pocket watch and said, "I'll answer one
question, then we really must go."

"Three. And real answers, not tricky ones."

"Two." He twitched. "These are not people you want to
keep waiting."

"It's a deal." What was my first question? I wanted to know
more about the contents of Aunt Pandora's letter, but I was
pretty sure he had no idea what she had written, so I settled for
asking, "How did you know I would need a ride at precisely the
time you came to get me?"

He smiled, suddenly looking more like a fox than a rabbit,
and I wished I had put more conditions on the answers. "When
you phoned me, you said you were leaving the next day. I
figured you wouldn't be able to drive all the way through and
would stay overnight somewhere near Kansas City. Estimating
you would leave KC around eight or nine, I calculated you
would arrive at Echo Springs between two and four. When you
still hadn't appeared by four-thirty, I went looking for you. I
thought perhaps you had gotten lost or had car trouble."

"Okay." His answer seemed fairly reasonable. If he were
just my aunt's lawyer, it would be a bit of a stretch for him to
mount a search party, but since he thought of himself as my
honorary uncle, I could understand him wanting to take care of
me.

Now what was my second question? I chewed my lip until it
came to me. "Why haven't you asked me where my car is?" I
could tell he was pleased with his last answer, but maybe this
would wipe that smirk off his face.

He smiled again, this time I could see some hyena in his
heritage. Taking my elbow, he said, "I saw the break in the
guardrail on the bridge, and figured your car must have gone into

the river." He moved me into the reception area. "I was relieved you hadn't gone over with it. I don't want to scare you, but if you had, we would probably have never found you. We have a saying around here. Whatever goes into the Ricochet River doesn't bounce back out."

Well, that was a relief. If the saying was true, my murderous ex-boyfriend was long gone. It was just a shame he'd taken my Camaro with him. "Aren't you curious as to why my car went off the bridge and how I got out?"

"Sorry. That was your third question," he smirked.

"But there was another vehicle involved." I realized that I probably should have mentioned Gil and the fact he and his Hummer had gone off the bridge earlier, then again, there was so much happening to me, it had nearly slipped my mind. "We need to notify the police."

"No problem." Uncle Will smirked again. "The Echo Springs police chief will be at the party."

At that, the bunny reappeared, and with his nose twitching, Uncle Will tugged me toward the outer door.

"Look, I'll go to the meet and greet, but shouldn't I change first?" I gestured to my jeans and sweatshirt.

"You look fine. We're pretty casual around here. Not like those highfalutin' city folks." He succeeded in getting me into his car and closed the passenger door on my protests.

After a short drive, during which I used a Wet One to wipe the dirt off my face, combed my hair, and put on some lipstick, we pulled into a spot in front of the restaurant he had pointed out earlier.

Uncle Will immediately hopped out of the Bentley, darted around the hood, and opened my door. He tugged me out of the car, pulled me up to ornate double doors with MIRAGE etched into the glass, then swept me inside.

Without giving me a chance to look around, he guided me

through the restaurant and into an enormous private room in the rear. Decorated in red velvet, brass, and mirrors, it reminded me of old-world mansions I had seen pictures of in travel books. That or a bordello. I'd seen pictures of those, too.

All conversation ceased as we walked in. They had set this area up for a cocktail party, with a bar and trays of hors d'oeuvres arranged on a long table along the back wall, and everyone stood in the center of the room facing us.

Crap! I knew I should have insisted on showering and changing clothes.

Most of the men were wearing suits, and the women had on what my mother used to call their Sunday best. They were all staring at me as if I had just crawled out from under a rock, which, to be fair, was how I looked.

I hissed at Uncle Will, "Why didn't you let me get fixed up? This is not casual."

"You're fine." Uncle Will glanced at someone I couldn't see and paled. His voice shook as he said, "Your appearance is the least of your worries."

What did he mean by that? I wasn't sure I wanted to find out. Maybe coming to Echo Springs hadn't been a good idea after all.

CHAPTER SIX
Possible Side Effects

I didn't have time to figure out what had caused Uncle Will's fearfulness because he immediately introduced me around. I forgot the names of most of the attendees as soon as we moved to the next person, but some were more memorable.

For instance, the guy in the jeans and leather jacket bore an uncanny resemblance to James Dean.

When Uncle Will introduced him as Jeremy Wilson, I waited for Will to mention something about the younger man's likeness to the doomed movie star, but all he said was, "Jeremy owns Wilson's Garage and Gas Station. He'll take care of Dora's vehicle for you, if you have any problems with it."

Problems? Oh, great, Aunt Dora's car was probably a 1978 Chevy Chevette or something equally ancient and awful.

While Jeremy seemed to be in his mid to late twenties, all ages were well represented among the attendees. From what I gathered, everyone at the party owned businesses in town, ranches on the outskirts, or were professionals such as the doctor, the president of the bank, and the high school principal. Undoubtedly they were Echo Spring's movers and shakers.

Take the next woman we approached.

Uncle Will put his hand on her arm and said, "This is Francine Althorp." He didn't blink as he introduced the Princess Diana lookalike. "She owns Althorp's Fine Apparel."

Although I was never a big fan of the ill-fated princess, my mother had loved her. Which meant that I had seen enough of the seemingly endless TV and magazine stories about her royal highness to recognize her short blond hair, distinctive nose, and big blue eyes.

She shook my hand and said in an upper-class British accent, "I hope you'll stop by my shop. We have some terribly nice things in larger sizes that would look super on you."

Larger sizes? I narrowed my eyes. Well, yes, I took a double-digit size, while she was probably a two on her worst, most bloated day, but did she have to mention it?

I squeezed her delicate hand, okay, maybe a little harder than I should have, and answered, "Thank you so much, Prin...er...Francine. I'll be sure to take you up on your kind offer sometime."

Yeah, when hell freezes over.

After we moved on, I whispered to Uncle Will, "Wasn't that James Dean and Princess Diana?"

"I'll explain later." He shook his head slightly. "Don't bring it up.

Hmmm. I ruminated through the next several introductions, then almost lost it when Uncle Will introduced me to the town mayor, Patrick Fitzgerald. Patrick was the spitting image of President John F. Kennedy. What was this place? A refuge for all the celebrities who died in automobiles?

I opened my mouth, but Uncle Will elbowed me in the ribs and hissed in my ear. "Don't ask."

Swallowing my original words, I said instead, "Nice to meet you, Mayor." I wonder what would have happened if I had greeted him with "Ich bin ein Echo Springer?"

Once again Uncle Will towed me away before I could have any kind of conversation with the mayor. This time we made it all the way to the rear of the room, where a woman in her late twenties and two men maybe a year or so older stood.

Uncle Will placed his hand on the woman's shoulder and said, "Alexandria, this is your cousin, Elissa Morningstar."

"Call me Lexie." I kept my expression neutral as I studied her.

She had curly red hair and mischievous green eyes, not quite beautiful, but certainly close enough that I would bet she could have any guy in town. We stared at each other. It was that moment when two women meet and decide whether they would be friends or competition. Seeing as she had on a luscious Kiwi-colored jersey dress and matching striped canvas wedges, she had me at a disadvantage.

A second later, she smiled and hugged me, whispering in my ear, "Come over to the library tomorrow around lunchtime so we can talk."

I nodded my consent, wondering what she wanted to talk about. Was it all the undead celebrities or the coincidences that brought me to Echo Springs? Or maybe it was about why my father had been murdered.

Probably not. With my luck, she just wanted to warn me that the two yummy males she was with were hers.

The men in question stood shoulder-to-shoulder, reminding me of the white and black kings from my ivory and ebony chessboard. A possession I had loved but had had to leave behind.

Uncle Will patted the dark-haired guy's biceps. "Alexandria, this is Lucas Furman. We passed his family's ranch on the way into town."

"How do you do?" I smiled at the Adonis standing before me and vowed to get even with my uncle for making me meet him looking like I had just stumbled out of a storm-ravaged sewer. "Please call me Lexie."

"My pleasure." He shook my hand, and I shivered.

You know that tingly feeling you get when you meet someone special? After my experiences with Gil, I now realize that prickle is your common sense leaving your body, so I ignored the warmth blossoming in my chest and gave him a cool smile.

But I couldn't ignore how well his massive shoulders filled his suit jacket or the inherent strength in his chiseled face. However, it was his compelling brown eyes that nearly mesmerized me.

People always commented on the variegations in my eyes, and his were the same configuration, only a dark honey and cinnamon in ocher, while mine were green and gold in amber. I had never seen anyone with a similar pattern to mine before.

Before I was ready, he let go of my hand, and the white king immediately claimed it. He was as tall as Lucas, and while leaner still nicely muscled.

Uncle Will said, "And this is Cole Pendergast, our host for the evening."

Blond hair and brows complemented his fair skin, and his features were nearly perfect. One more degree of delicacy and they would have made him too beautiful for a man.

He drew me closer, and said something charming, but I didn't hear the words because once again, I was staring at eyes that were patterned like my own. Only this time they were sky blue and indigo in silver.

What in the heaven's name was going on here?

There had been a definite spark when Lucas had taken my hand and another when Cole touched me. Now, as Cole murmured in my ear about getting to know one another better, Lucas stepped closer and took my other hand.

As soon as skin touched skin, there was a flash, and warmth surged from my toes to the top of my head. The hair on my arms stood up, and the air in front of me looked wavy. Out of nowhere, an older woman with a copper and gray-streaked bun materialized.

Eyes that matched mine exactly stared at me, and I heard her say, "Choose carefully."

Just before everything went black, I yelled, "What? Choose

what?"

I don't know how long I was out, but as I fought my way toward consciousness, I heard someone whisper, "We have to kill her before she comes into her full powers."

I was pretty sure they were talking about me and with a moan, I slipped back into the darkness.

CHAPTER SEVEN
To The Magic Born

I was still lying on the restaurant floor when I came to the second time. For someone who had never fainted before, lately, I was sure spending a lot of time out cold.

At least I wasn't keeling over for trivial reasons. In two days, two separate people with two different bizarre reasons wanted me dead. That had to be some kind of record.

When I finally pried open my reluctant eyelids, I saw a pack of Echo Springs' leading citizens hovering over me like jackals around a downed antelope. Keeping a wary eye on the people crowded around me, I struggled to a sitting position. Once I was upright, I stared hard at each one of them attempting to determine who had been casually discussing my murder. Surely they weren't all in on it.

At least I hoped not. Because if they were, I was as dead as a mouse in a trap. And I hadn't even been allowed to eat the tasty cheese yet.

"Alexandria, stay still, my dear." Evidently, Uncle Will had been talking to me while I was trying to figure out who was planning my imminent demise, because he let out a little sigh and said slowly, as if he were waiting for my brain to get back from its holiday, "Let Dr. Silvia examine you."

"No." I shook my head, fending off a well-dressed woman in her late thirties who was trying to take my pulse. "Thank you, doctor, but I'm fine."

Dr. Silvia pushed her bangs out of her solemn brown eyes and said, "If you lose consciousness again, you need to come to see me immediately."

"Will do."

Elissa nudged Uncle Will out of her way bent toward me, and asked, "Are you sure you're all right?"

"Yes." Struggling to my feet, I added, "I just need a minute to regroup."

Elissa glanced at Uncle Will who shrugged, then lent me a hand. As soon as I was on my feet, I pushed my way out of the throng and zoomed into the ladies' room with Elissa hot on my heels. She locked the door behind her and watched silently as I stepped up to the mirror.

One glimpse of my reflection convinced me not to take a second glance. When I had arrived at the dinner, I had already looked like I'd been cleaning toilets, and the time I had spent on the floor hadn't improved my appearance.

There was little I could do to make myself look better except wash my face, smooth my hair, and brush off my clothes. What I really needed was a shower, a set of electric curlers, and some serious time with my makeup case.

Elissa didn't say a word as I used the facilities, then washed my hands, but as I stood there shredding a paper towel, she asked, "Ready to go back?"

Unable to think of any other reason to delay my return to the dining room, I took a deep breath and nodded. Elissa hooked her elbow with mine, and we returned to the lions' den.

I got through the rest of the evening without any further crises, but as soon as the meal was finished, I whispered to Uncle Will, "Get me out of here."

He started to argue, but the expression on my face must have convinced him that either I could walk out of the room now, or he could carry me out later, because he made our excuses and drove me to my new residence.

Uncle Will kept stealing little peeks at me as he steered the big car down dimly lit streets. He was probably surprised I wasn't peppering him with questions about all I had seen and heard at the dinner, but I was too tired to start an interrogation. Tomorrow would be soon enough to pry some answers out of him.

I'm not sure what I had been expecting, but the pale lemon three-story home with the gingerbread trim and wraparound porch was not it, and I shuddered. It might have been a beautiful house, but it was also the one I had been having dreams about since I was six years old. How could I possibly have known about this place?

Refusing to be creeped out, I concentrated on the positives. Once Uncle Will knew I was coming, he'd had someone clean the place and stock the fridge, and when we walked inside the pleasant odor of lemon furniture wax greeted us.

After he'd helped me with my luggage, Uncle Will handed me the key, kissed me on the cheek, and said, "Remember, Chief Neville wants to speak to you tomorrow at three about your accident. He gave you his card, right?"

"Uh-huh," I mumbled, too tired to say much else.

"And when you're finished at the police station, we need to finish up the paperwork for your inheritance. Call me if you need anything." Uncle Will patted my shoulder and started to leave, but stopped and added, "Elissa lives in the cottage a little ways down the lane, so don't be alarmed if you see a car turn into the drive."

"Okay." I wondered how my cousin felt about me inheriting the estate but didn't have the energy to ask. Instead, I said, "Thanks for everything."

Then barely waiting until Uncle Will was out the door, I locked it and leaned against the wall. The wave of exhaustion I had been fighting hit me like a tsunami, and the staircase to the second floor looked like Mt. Everest.

There was no way I could make that climb without the

assistance of a couple of Sherpas. And since none seemed to be available, I looked around for another alternative.

A brief examination of the first floor revealed that Aunt Pandora had converted a back parlor into a master suite and I blessed her for doing so as I collapsed on the bed.

* * *

The next morning I woke from a deep, dreamless sleep knowing exactly where I was. Which was odd, as was the fact that the memory of my life in Chicago was already fading. I could barely recall my employer's name.

Stretching, I realized that I felt amazingly good—especially considering Gil's attack, the car accident, and my fainting episode. I should have been bruised and battered, but I couldn't locate even the tiniest ache or pain.

Hmm! Speaking of passing out, what exactly had happened when I collapsed? In the light of day, I was less willing to believe that the mere touch of two men had made me keel over or that the Echo Springs' upper crust was plotting to kill me, much less that my dead aunt had spoken to me from beyond the grave.

I was halfway to convincing myself that I had passed out because of low blood sugar, and that the rest was only a dream when I spotted the portrait above the fireplace. It was of a woman who looked a lot like me. Same copper-colored hair, same variegated eyes, same curvy figure.

Fast-forward thirty years or so, and the woman in the picture would resemble the one I had seen just before I lost consciousness. I had never met my aunt, so how had I known what she looked like?

When I couldn't think of a logical explanation, I told myself that I had too much to do, to worry about a silly hypoglycemic dream. Among other things, I needed to explore the house, unpack, and get some answers from my cousin and honorary uncle.

The master suite included an attached bathroom which was deliciously sumptuous. The whirlpool tub was big enough to require a lifeguard, and the separate shower was so large I could have fit the entire bathroom from my apartment inside its tiled walls.

It seemed my aunt, and I shared a taste for the good things in life. However, unlike me, it appeared she could afford them. Maybe I had inherited more than I thought.

After showering, I did my hair and makeup and dressed in crisp khakis, a primrose oxford shirt, and my favorite Gucci loafers. Feeling more like myself, and thus back in control, I investigated the kitchen.

In the refrigerator, I found a package of Multigrain Light Thomas's English muffins, real butter, orange marmalade, and sugar-free French vanilla creamer, which were exactly my breakfast items of choice. How could someone have known that? Another question for Uncle Will.

Rested, fed, and sipping my second cup of Godiva chocolate truffle coffee, I was ready to survey my new surroundings. A front parlor faced the street. It was furnished in delicate antiques and looked as if no one had set foot on the exquisite Oriental carpet in a couple of decades.

Opposite the parlor was a combination study/den/family room, which must have been where my aunt had spent her time. A comfortably-worn leather sofa and matching chair were arranged around an oval braided rug. Built-in bookshelves occupied two walls, and a large desk with a computer took up most of a third. On the remaining wall, facing the couch was a fireplace with a flat screen TV mounted above it.

All the surfaces were dust free and sparkled. Whoever Uncle Will had hired to clean the place had done a fantastic job. Was she available on a permanent basis? More importantly, could I afford her?

Making a mental note to ask him the housekeeper's name, I moved on. The dining room echoed the style and perfection of the parlor, but I had noted earlier that the kitchen had been modernized with stainless steel appliances, cherry wood cabinets, and gorgeous black quartz counters.

The back parlor that had been remodeled to serve as the master suite was next on my tour. The stone fireplace on the wall opposite the bed seemed to be the only remnant of the old room.

An interesting picture of my aunt was emerging. She was a woman with ties to both the old and the new—and money enough to buy what she wanted. That had to be a good sign, right?

Checking my watch, I saw it was only ten o'clock. There was plenty of time to investigate the second floor. Except, when I climbed the stairs, I couldn't get into any of the four rooms lining the upstairs hallway. The doors were all dead-bolted, and none of the keys Uncle Will had left me worked.

I could understand Aunt Pandora's desire to save on gas and electricity by closing up those rooms. She was a single person occupying a large house. But why did she lock them?

Curiously, I mounted the small spiral staircase to the third floor, but the entrance leading to this area was bolted, as well. Before I could do anything about clearing out the house, I needed to find the keys to all these locked doors. Maybe Uncle Will had them.

Not wanting to miss my lunch date with Elissa, I decided to unpack my suitcases would take less time than going through my aunt's desk and file cabinet. Unfortunately, a quick peek revealed that Pandora's clothes still occupied the walk-in closet and dresser drawers.

What should I do with them? Not only was I uncomfortable handling the intimate apparel of someone I had never met, but it also seemed disrespectful to throw them away.

Briefly, I considered asking my cousin for her help but dismissed the thought. Elissa had seemed friendly enough, but what if she resented the fact that I had inherited Aunt Pandora's estate? Or was she related to me from my mother's side of the family? *I definitely need to see a family tree.*

In the end, I decided to pack up my aunt's things and ask Uncle Will if he had a suggestion on what to do with them. There were several flattened boxes and a roll of packing tape in the screened-in back porch. After assembling the cartons, I filled them with the contents of the closet and drawers.

Aunt Pandora had had eclectic tastes, running the style gamut from Lee jeans to Chanel suits. Her shoes where mostly practical and there were only three handbags—all original Coach shoulder bags. One in black, one in brown, and one in cream.

The only unusual item I found was in the nightstand. It was a large wooden box with a lid that flipped up by pulling on a satin tab. Inside were three separate compartments—each holding one item. The two smaller ones contained a lock of ebony hair tied with a red ribbon and a tiny wooden piano with both the white and black keys carefully carved. The third held a mother-of-pearl backed mirror. Something told me to leave them where they were.

The packing and unpacking had taken me longer than I thought, and it was already well past noon before I glanced at the bedside clock. *Shoot!* I didn't want Elissa to think I had stood her up.

At least I was already dressed. I ran a comb through my hair, freshened my lipstick, and picked up my purse.

Earlier I had noticed a set of car keys hanging from a hook in the kitchen. Grabbing them on my way out, I crossed a small stretch of lawn and opened the garage's pedestrian door.

Pandora's car was a pleasant surprise. Instead of an

oldladymobile, it was a cute little red pickup truck. However, my smile faded when I saw that it was a stick shift.

The last time I had driven anything but an automatic was when I was seventeen. A boy in the trailer park my mother and I were living in at the time had an old VW Beetle with a manual transmission. In exchange for a few kisses, he taught me how to drive it. But that was over twelve years ago, and I wasn't sure how well I remember those lessons.

Evidently not that well. In the mile or so to the library, I stalled the truck three times, and that didn't count all the tries it took me to back out of the garage.

When I finally arrived, I briefly considered a spot right in front, but it required parallel parking, and I knew my limitations. Instead, I chose a pull-through slot in the rear lot.

By the time I hurried up the concrete steps of the two-story white stone building, it was already a quarter to one. I could only hope lunchtime in Echo Springs wasn't strictly at noon.

The person behind the counter couldn't have been much over twenty or so. Her hair was dyed a hot pink and stuck up from her head like a rooster's comb, revealing the tattoo of a feather under her ear curling around her neck and disappearing down her shirt collar. Not exactly what I expected for a small town librarian.

Without lifting her eyes from the book in front of her, and before I could ask for my cousin, she pointed to a flight of stairs and said, "Go down, first door on your left."

Thinking she had me confused with someone else, I said, "Uh, I'm here to see Elissa Morningstar."

"Right. Down the stairs, first door on your left."

Since I'd arrived in Echo Springs, the hair on the back of my neck had been getting a real workout. I was having more and more trouble finding a rational explanation for all the weird things happening to me, and it was becoming harder and harder to stay afloat in the river of denial. But I wasn't ready to dive into that water yet, so, I told myself that Elissa had described me to the girl and told her I was coming.

The library was old, and while the upstairs had been well maintained, the basement was dank and smelled musty. Elissa's office was a little better. She had painted it a tranquil sea green, hung travel posters framed to look like windows, and had a diffuser with a pleasant lavender scent sitting on top of a filing cabinet.

But it was Elissa's own effervescent personality and attractiveness that transformed the space from grim to inviting. Today she was wearing a white cotton skirt with a crocheted hem and a tangerine striped tunic. Once again, I felt underdressed.

She jumped up when she spotted me and gave me a big hug. "Lexie, have you recovered from last night?"

I stiffened. "Yes. I'm fine." I wasn't really a touchy-feely person, and in the fashion world, the hugs and kisses consisted more of air-to-air than actual flesh-to-flesh. "I'm sure it was just a combination of hunger and exhaustion."

"Sure."

"I drove from Kansas City and didn't stop for lunch," I elaborated.

Elissa raised an eyebrow, but didn't comment. She indicated a chair pulled close to her desk, and after I sat, she reached down and picked up a large square basket with a red gingham napkin covering the top. "Since we have so much to talk about, I thought it would be better if we ate here where we could have some privacy."

"Great." I looked at her expectantly, happy to have any of the hundreds of questions jumping around in my head answered. It made me nervous when she remained silent, so I blurted out, "I was surprised the library was open on a Sunday, most of the ones in Chicago aren't."

"You'll find things here are a lot different than in the city," Elissa chuckled.

"I'm sure. So how about telling me all about my new hometown?"

She opened her mouth and closed it a couple of times before sighing. It looked to me like my cousin couldn't figure out where to begin.

Finally, she asked, "Are you looking forward to taking over the store?"

"Actually, I've been thinking about that." On my way over to the library, it had dawned on me that with Gil dead and the money from my inheritance, I really didn't have to stick around Echo Springs. I could live anywhere. Judging from Aunt Pandora's house, there could even be enough cash for me to go back to grad school. "I might sell the business and finish my doctorate."

"No!" Elissa squealed, then took a deep breath, and said in a soothing tone, as if she was talking to someone about to leap off a rooftop, "You mustn't do that."

"Why not?" My cousin's reaction seemed a tad much. We'd only met yesterday. Why did she care what I did? "Uncle Will didn't mention anything about any conditions of my inheritance."

"No, technically, there aren't any." Elissa wrinkled her brow. "But no one but a Ravenscraft can own the candy store."

"I'd be happy to sell it to someone in the family."

I was willing to let my relatives have first dibs as long as they paid me a fair price. I'd have to find someone who could appraise the store for me and tell me how much it was worth. "I'm afraid there's only Mother and me, and we aren't the heir."

Mentally, I slapped myself upside the head. I had to stop being so impulsive. I shouldn't have revealed my intentions to sell the business until I knew more about what was going on. My luck, Elissa and her mother would contest Aunt Pandora's will if they thought I wouldn't run the candy store myself.

"You're right," I quickly backpedaled. "I guess I should settle in and see how things go before I decide."

"Terrific." She took a crisp white cloth from the picnic basket and spread it on the desktop, then laid knives, forks, and plates in front of us. "How about we have some lunch while I give you a run-down on the family?"

I nodded and pulled a notepad and pen out of my purse. "That would be great."

She unscrewed the lid of a thermos, poured iced tea into two glasses, and gave me one, then took a sip from hers before continuing. "Your father, Nathanial, and my mother, Nora, were twins. Both of their parents were killed in an automobile accident when they were babies, and their father's sister, Pandora raised them."

"So you and I are first cousins on the Ravenscraft side. And you don't have any siblings?" When Elissa shook her head no, I asked, "Are your parents still alive?"

"Yes. You would have met them last night, but they're visiting my dad's family. They'll be back in a couple of days."

"Terrific." I was excited to meet more of the family I hadn't known existed.

"The thing is," Elissa put out a plate of sandwiches and a bowl of fruit and motioned me to help myself, "Ravenscrafts seldom produce more than one offspring, so the twins were a rarity and an opportunity for the family to increase. But my mother only had me. And, well, your father..."

"Was killed." I completed her sentence as I selected a turkey on what looked like homemade bread and scooped some fruit salad onto my plate.

"Yes. There was never a chance to see if he would have had

more children."

"How did it happen? Who did it?" I asked, then took a bite of the sandwich.

"He was stabbed in the heart, in his driveway the night before your birth. They have never found his killer."

"Is that why my mother took me away and changed her name?"

"Miranda wasn't one of us. Your father had met her when he was away from town. She never really understood his position or accepted yours." Elissa popped a grape into her mouth.

"I see." Having no idea what my dad's position was or why being from out of town made it hard to comprehend, I really didn't see, but I didn't want to interrupt Elissa's train of thought.

"We think Miranda was afraid whoever murdered Nathanial would kill her and you too, so she ran away and severed her connection with Echo Springs." Elissa shrugged. "But we're not sure. Although Aunt Pandora kept an eye on both of you, she never spoke to your mother."

"How did Pandora keep an eye on us?" I ate a chunk of watermelon.

"I'll get to that, but first I need to tell you more about our family."

"Why didn't Aunt Pandora leave everything to you or at least divide it between us?"

Elissa took a deep breath and said, "It's time to tell you more about our family's unusual gifts."

"Like what?"

"Like what Aunt Pandora was referring to when she wrote that you were a special person destined to hold many lives in your hands."

"You saw her letter to me?"

"I saw the words, but Aunt Pandora didn't show the actual letter to me," she answered, then continued, "You are the eldest

Ravenscraft of our generation, which means you inherit the bulk of our power."

"Power?" That sounded good. Power usually meant wealth. Maybe the estate was worth a lot more than I initially thought.

"Our magic."

"Darn." Was she serious? "I was hoping for cash." I thought she would laugh and say she had been teasing, but she didn't.

Instead, she asked, "Haven't you noticed that you have a special ability? You're able to sense what people want? What they really need?"

"I..." Slamming my mouth shut, I shook my head. "Of course not."

"Really?" Elissa stared into my eyes and said, "Tell the truth."

Although I had no intention of doing so, I found myself admitting, "Okay, sort of, but it's not magic."

"Of course it is." Elissa smiled at me as if I were a three-year-old denying that I was potty trained. "If you had been raised here, this would be soooo much easier."

I rolled my eyes. "So I just twitch my nose? Is that it?"

She ignored my taunt and said, "I hate to do this to you but..." She stared into my eyes again. "Tell me about your last experience involving your ability. Start at the beginning and tell me the whole story."

"Uh." I didn't want to tell her. I didn't want to spill my guts to a stranger, even if we were cousins, but the words just trickled out of me. "The past few years I've been working at this chichi boutique in Chicago as a fashion consultant. Not that being a salesclerk was ever my life's goal, but when my mom got sick while I was in graduate school, I needed the money for her bills."

Whoa! I never told anyone about this stuff. I didn't want people feeling sorry for me. Why was I telling her?

"I understand." Elissa patted my hand. "Family always

comes first. Go on."

"Anyway," I leaned back out of her reach. It was almost as if every time she touched me, our connection grew stronger and if I ever want to leave Echo Springs that might not be a good thing. "...as it turned out..." I continued my story until I reached the part about being fired.

"That wasn't your ability's fault." Elissa's tone brooked no argument. "It was just time for you to come home. Remember what Aunt Pandora wrote. You would only receive her letter when two events came to pass. She died, and you were at the point in your life when you needed to know the truth about yourself. No matter when she died, you would not have read her note until the second condition was met."

"Right," I sneered, although a tiny part of me was beginning to believe.

"Try to keep an open mind," Elissa sighed. "Our family has solved the mysteries and protected the magical community for hundreds of years. Since the day we arrived in Echo Springs from the old country, the candy store has been the conduit by which we provide our assistance."

"How?" I had completely lost my appetite and put my mostly untouched plate aside.

"Think of it being like a sheriff in a small town. We investigate the complaint, decide what's required, and give out what's needed."

"Of course we do." I didn't bother to hide the sarcasm in my voice.

"Surely you've noticed that unusual things happen around you," Elissa said. "Even before the incident that got you sacked."

Rather than admit that I did seem to have a higher than average tendency to attract the bizarre, I asked, "Who or what do we protect the magical community from?"

"I guess you could call it the corrupt magic. The kind that's intended to harm rather than to help. The kind that's used for personal gain." Elissa leaned forward. "In nature, there is always a light and a dark side, and we try to maintain that balance. The other families in town are torn between the two. Each generation must choose its own path, so it's never clear who can be trusted."

"But not the Ravenscrafts?" The rational half of me was asking why I was still sitting there. "We have to choose the good side?"

Elissa looked surprised at my question, and thought for a moment before saying, "We always have, so, based on history, I'd say yes."

"Then the Ravenscrafts are Wiccan?"

"No, we're Catholic." She wrinkled her nose, "And we don't like the word witch either."

Her response surprised me, and it took a few seconds to process why, then I sputtered, "How can you go to church and still believe this good and evil magic...stuff?" I almost said crap, but that seemed needlessly rude.

"How can I not?" Elissa's expression was grim. "I'm one of the few who truly comprehends what would happen if God and his churches weren't around. During the times when the corrupt magic is dominant, those who believe in Him resist the wickedness, allowing the world to survive until good is back in control."

That made sense. Well, as much sense as anything else she had said.

"So, is there a head honcho of the evil side?" I asked.

"Yes.

"Who?" I blurted out.

If I believed any of this nonsense, there'd been a few people I'd met last night who seemed like they might be prime candidates. Especially the person I'd overheard plotting my death.

"No one ever knows until the battle is won."

"The battle for what?" Was she kidding?

"Power." Elissa's tone was utterly serious. "We try to keep the balance tipped in favor of the helpful magic. He tries to swing it toward the harmful kind."

"You said he. Is it a man?"

"Not necessarily."

"While this all sounds fascinating." I squirmed in my seat, wondering why I was even listening to this nonsense. "It's really not for me, so..."

Elissa gently cut me off and continued, "As the Ravenscraft Shield you have certain obligations and duties. The primary ones are to produce the next Ravenscraft Shield. Meanwhile, you need to protect yourself from the master of the corrupt magic who will try to steal your abilities. And, once you figured out who the leader is, you need to capture his powers."

"How does one take another person's magic?"

My only cousin was nuttier than a Snickers bar, but she certainly knew how to keep my interest. Maybe she was writing a book and testing the plot out on me.

Elissa bit her lip. "The Ravenscraft Shield does it by finding the correct charm." At my questioning look, she explained, "Charms are how our most important magic works."

"And the bad guy?" I had a feeling his method wouldn't be quite so civilized.

"He can also use an instrument of his power, but he'll most likely kill you."

"Not that I believe any of this." Although I should have fled Elissa's office screaming by now, curiosity had me rooted to my seat. "But for the sake of argument, why doesn't the bad guy just do away with me right now, before I have a baby, etcetera, etcetera?"

"Because he can't acquire your magic until you are in full

possession of all your powers and that doesn't happen until the next heir is born." Elissa looked me in the eye. "But if it looks as if you're a threat to him before this occurs, he'll cut his losses, and kill you even if he can't seize your magic."

"Great." I foolishly asked another question, "What happens to my magic if I die before the bad guy can steal it?"

"If you die before you come into full possession of your magic, Mother becomes the Shield. If you die after you've come into your powers and have taken away the magic from the bad guy, we wait for the next Shield to come into his or her maturity. In the case of your father, that was you."

"Not your mom?" I rose from my chair and edged toward the door. I needed to leave before I said something I'd regret— like suggest she see a psychiatrist.

"No. Most of the Ravenscraft magic reverted to Aunt Pandora. It always goes to the eldest Ravenscraft alive if the Shield dies. But Aunt Pandora wasn't able to reclaim it all. That's why she could keep track of your mother, but couldn't force her to return home."

"Okay, then." I put my hand on the doorknob and turned it. "Nice fairy tale, but I really have a lot to do. You know, to settle in and all."

"I recognize the things I'm telling you seem unbelievable, but they are very real." Elissa ignored my words. "Didn't you think it was odd that you couldn't find Echo Springs on a map or GPS or the Internet? And that the road leading here wasn't there the first time you looked?" She must have seen the answer on my face because she continued, "The townspeople use their magic to keep Echo Springs hidden from outsiders. The only way any non-Echo Springians can get into town is if they are escorted by one of us. And if someone does that without the approval of the council, they are stripped of their abilities and banished."

"Right. We have to keep the humans from finding out about

the magic. Good thing my ex-boyfriend drove his Hummer off the bridge before he tried to get into town."

"Yes, it was." Elissa didn't seem at all shocked to hear what I'd just said. Maybe Uncle Will had filled her in on the accident.

"Uh, thank you for lunch." *Darn.* I would have liked to have a cousin to be close to, but this one was clearly insane. "You'll have to let me cook for you sometime." Like as soon as my elven housekeeper appeared.

Elissa went on as if I hadn't spoken. "The townspeople all still possess abilities, no one without them can live here. But some families have faded, or for some reason, a generation kept the information from their descendants, and they don't know about their powers." Elissa frowned. "One of these you should look out for is the police chief. He is aware of his heritage, but ignores it most of the time." She chewed on her thumbnail. "Aunt Pandora never told me why."

Elissa got up and walked over to where I stood. "Let me ask you something before you go. Do you like to read?"

"Yes." Was she going to offer me a library card?

"Fiction?"

"Yes."

"Isn't it true in order to enjoy fiction, you have to be able to suspend belief?"

I nodded.

"This is the same thing. In order for you to survive and succeed in your calling as the Ravenscraft Shield, you must accept that things you can't see, things you can't prove, exist."

"Uh huh." Right. "Well, it's been nice talking to you." I pasted a phony smile on my face and edged into the hallway.

"You'll see," Elissa said as I backed away. "No one escapes their true destiny."

CHAPTER EIGHT
Crimes and Witch-Demeanors

Once I made it out of the library, I sat behind the wheel of Aunt Pandora's truck and shook my head. A giggle bubbled to the surface, then another and another, until I was laughing so hard tears ran down my cheeks.

Magic! Did Elissa really believe we could do magic? And not just the Ravenscrafts, but also the whole town?

Wait until Uncle Will heard about this. He'd probably tell me she was a huge practical joker. Or was giving me a hard time because she didn't inherit. Or even that she was just plain batty. Maybe that was why he'd been leery about me meeting her today.

Yesterday, when he'd warned me about getting too cozy with anyone, including Elissa, I'd thought he was paranoid. I could understand him cautioning me about the rest of Echo Springs' citizens, but not my own cousin. Now I reconsidered my opinion.

Satisfied that I had figured things out, and refusing to think about why I had told Elissa about my so-called ability when I had been determined not to reveal it, I looked at my watch. It was only one-forty-five, and I didn't have to meet with the police chief until three.

This was as good a time as any to brush up my stick shift skills. And I could acquaint myself with my new hometown while I practiced. I needed to buy a cell phone to replace the one I'd left in my apartment back in Chicago. I'd also keep an eye out for a beauty salon—I wanted a professional to shape the hack job that I'd done on my hair. A real estate office was the third item on my list. Elissa's craziness had made me even more determined to sell Aunt Pandora's properties and return to grad school.

Putting the truck into gear, I slowly drove out of the library's parking lot and headed for Echo Springs' main drag. In addition to the businesses I'd seen last night when Uncle Will drove me through town, today I noticed the Wizard of Hog, a cute little diner, a bookstore called Spellbound Books, and craft shop by the name Wish Upon a Hobby.

Either Elissa's nonsense was getting to me, or all the merchants along the main street had agreed to a magical theme for their business names.

My head was starting to pound, so I turned at the first corner and maneuvered aimlessly through the residential streets. Thankfully, all the houses seemed ordinary, and I could relax and concentrate on relearning how to drive a manual transmission.

The next time I checked the time it was five to three. *Shit!* Chief Neville hadn't struck me as a man you wanted to keep waiting.

At least I was already in town and had located the police station on my trip down the main street. In the mile or so to the station, I used one hand to apply some lipstick and smooth my hair, which was sticking up all over my head. Evidently, I had been running my fingers through it while I drove.

With my renewed confidence in my stick shift ability, I took the spot right in front of the PD, parallel parking the truck on my first try. As soon as it was snuggled between a Lincoln Continental and a Ford minivan, I hopped out and jogged up the sidewalk to the front door.

It was a minute after three. By the time I hurried up the concrete steps of the two-story white stone building. I could only hope Chief Neville's watch was running late.

The young woman behind the reception desk was drop dead gorgeous. Her hair was platinum blond and clung to her head in a perfect pixie cut.

Instead of a uniform, she wore a pink skaters skirt and a cropped floral T-shirt. Hardly what I'd have pictured for a small-town police dispatcher, but maybe she was just a part-timer filling in on Sundays when no one else wanted to work.

She smiled at me with twin dimples and asked, "Can I help you?"

"Alexandria Ravenscraft to see Chief Neville."

Her impossibly blue eyes sparkled, and she held out her hand, "I'm Faylynn. I wanted to meet you last night, but my father wouldn't take me with him to the party."

"You didn't miss much." I winked as I shook her hand. "Except me passing out."

"Oh, you poor thing. My cousin Lucas said he could see that you were plumb tuckered out." Faylynn squeezed my fingers sympathetically. "I don't know why they couldn't let you rest before welcoming you to town."

"Me either." My cheeks warmed at the thought of Lucas talking about me. I wanted to ask if he said anything else, but shoved away that silly notion and said, "Uh, I really shouldn't keep the chief waiting."

"Right." She stepped over to the stairs and shouted, "Dad, Alexandria, is here!"

"Call me Lexie." I smiled at her and then asked, "Should I go up?"

"Sure. First door on your left." Faylynn touched my arm as I passed her. "Don't let my father scare you. His bark is worse than his bite." She tilted her head. "At least this time of the month."

What did she mean by that? Did the chief suffer from a male version of PMS?

The police station was old, and while the main floor looked as if it hadn't been remodeled in the past fifty years, the second story appeared to have just had a full-sized facelift. The chief's office took up half the space and was a painted a warm cocoa with massive oak and leather furnishings.

Chief Neville was a big man, with thinning white hair, and a head that resembled a buffalo. He was behind his desk, frowning at an open folder when I walked through his door. He glanced pointedly at his watch before gesturing for me to sit down.

Once I was seated in a burgundy wing chair, he said, "So, you had a little mishap yesterday?"

"Well..." I wondered what he'd consider a major accident. "It was more than just a fender bender. My ex-boyfriend tried to run me off the road and ended up crashing his Hummer through the bridge rail and into the river."

"Will said that was what you told him." Chief Neville's silvery-gray eyes stared into mine. "But are you sure that's what happened? Could your boyfriend have been driving too fast trying to catch up with you, lost control of his vehicle, then panicked and driven off after pushing your car into the water?"

"No." I shook my head. "He'd already tried to kill me once before. He meant to shove my Camaro into the river. It was just lucky that I got out." The memory of the arrowhead I was clutching just before I escaped from my car made me glance at my palm. The triangular shaped burn was gone. "He was already arrested once for assaulting me. You can check with the Chicago police."

"All in due time." Chief Neville's voice held a trace of derision. "Why don't you tell me why you think this ex of yours wanted to kill you?"

"Uh." I stopped to gather my thoughts. "I'm not sure where to begin."

"Tell me everything." He leaned back, his big leather desk

chair creaking. "Don't leave anything out."

"I guess the whole thing started even before I broke up with him. Gil was an attorney with a prestigious law firm, and to say he was intense would be like comparing the temperature of molten lava to that of cheese fondue."

I waited for the chief to chuckle, but he didn't even crack a smile. Instead, he motioned for me to keep going.

When I didn't start talking right away, Chief Neville sneered, "Are you sure you broke up with him rather than vice versa?"

"Yes." I nodded. "And it surprised me that it upset him."

"Why is that?"

"I didn't think he felt that way about me." I shrugged. "It seemed as if we were just drifting along because neither of us had met anyone better."

"So although you were in a committed relationship, you were still looking?"

"No! That's not what I meant." I stared at the chief. I hadn't said Gil and I were exclusive. "All I meant is that if I'd known Gil's feelings for me were that strong, I'd have handled things differently."

"Right," the chief scoffed. "Like marrying him without a prenup, then in a year or two divorcing him and grabbing all his money."

Oh-oh. Had some gold-digger taken Chief Neville to the cleaners?

Ignoring his sarcasm, I said, "I would have never married him." I hurriedly continued when the chief raised a skeptical brow. "It had been at least a month since we'd had any communication, but then, out of the blue, Gil showed up at my door."

"And you let him in and made him think you were taking him back?" The chief glared at me. "You probably made him supper and had sex with him."

"No!" *Damn!* This guy had issues. "He broke into my apartment." I felt my cheeks turn red as I admitted, "I had forgotten to put on the deadbolt and chain, and he forced the lock."

"Did you call the police?" Chief Neville asked, but I could tell he suspected the answer was no.

"Not then, but I did later. I didn't want to bother the police if I could handle it myself." My hands were suddenly cold, and I clasped them together for warmth. "I asked Gil what he was doing in my apartment, and he said he'd come to take me to dinner. But something was off about him, so I kept my distance."

"Is that when you called 911?" Again, it was apparent the chief guessed that I hadn't.

"Not right at that moment," I hedged. "I told Gil I didn't feel that way about him anymore and didn't want to date him. I asked him to go. But instead of leaving, he pulled out a pistol and said that the only way he'd ever get over me was if I were dead."

"Right," Chief Neville snorted. "Because you're so beautiful. Or have you recently gained weight?"

I ignored the chief's dig at my size and continued, "Then Gil tried to kidnap me."

"So, how did you get away?" The chief still seemed doubtful.

I rubbed the goose bumps that had popped up on my arms. "I pretended to faint, and while Gil was distracted getting a roll of duct tape started, I grabbed a wrought iron lamp from the end table and hit him."

"Was that when you got out of the apartment?" The chief asked.

"No." My cheeks got even redder. Boy was I dumb. I hadn't even thought of running out the door. "I ran for my cell and dialed 911. But before my call was answered, Gil tackled me. I managed to get my hand free, and I snatched a letter opener from my skirt pocket. Then I waited until he pulled me towards him, and instead of resisting, I shoved myself upward with all my strength, slammed my head into his nose, and plunged the letter opener into his chest. But a second later he came at me again."

"And yet you're still here," Chief Neville taunted. "How is that?"

"Before he got to me someone pounded on the front door. It popped open because Gil had messed it up when he broke in. When Gil saw my neighbor standing there, he ran out. But he yelled that it wasn't over and he'd be back." I shivered, then added, "The police arrested him and held him overnight. I thought I had gotten out of town before he made bail, but evidently not."

"You tell quite a story." Chief Neville heaved himself to his feet and walked around the desk, stopping inches from my knees. "But things don't add up."

"Like what?" I felt intimidated with him looming over me, but he was too close for me to stand.

"First," the chief held up one sausage-like finger, "there is no sign that any car other than your Camaro crashed through the bridge rail."

"But—"

He cut me off, "Second, the Chicago police have no record of your supposed 911 call."

"I don't under—"

Chief Neville cut me off again, "And third, there is no trace of a Gil Osborn ever having been arrested or held in jail."

My mouth dropped open. The police had told me they had arrested Gil for domestic violence.

"In fact," Chief Neville broke into my racing thoughts, "there's no documentation that an Alexandria Ravenscraft ever lived in Chicago, or anywhere else for that matter."

Oops! Should I tell him that until yesterday that hadn't been my name? With Gil dead, there was no reason to keep it secret, but a part of me sensed informing him about what had brought me to Echo Springs wasn't a good idea.

I could just picture the chief rolling his eyes when I told him about the package I received from Aunt Pandora.

"Uh, well, you see," I hesitated, then blurted out, "I used a stage name in Chicago, Lexie Green."

It was the best excuse for my dual identity I could come up with at such short notice.

"You were an actress?" He leaned against his desktop and raised a skeptical brow. "Aren't you a little," he made an exaggerated curvy figure in the air, "to be in show business."

Grr! He'd implied that I was fat, again. It was a good thing he was the chief of police or I would have slapped him. "I was trying to be one." Crossing my legs, I hoped to appear relaxed. "I never had much luck."

"Your use of an alias doesn't explain why your boyfriend was never in jail as you claimed."

"You need to check again. Unless the cops lied to me or Gil pulled some strings to make the whole incident disappear, he was definitely arrested."

Chief Neville stared at me before straightening and picking up the phone. He ordered Faylynn to call the Chicago police and re-verify Gil's lack of incarceration. Once he hung up, he asked, "Is there anything else I can do for you?"

"As a matter of fact, there is." Aunt Pandora's letter had told me to follow my instincts, "I want you to look into my father's murder."

All expression drained from the chief's face, and he said, "That happened nearly thirty years ago. It's a cold case, and unless something new comes to light, there's nothing to investigate." He turned his back on me. "Now, I have another appointment, so you'll have to excuse me."

Apparently our meeting was over, and as I left the police station, I wondered what had just happened. Why had Chief Neville almost thrown me out of his office when I brought up my father's murder? And it didn't make sense that there wasn't any trace of Gil's Hummer on the bridge rail, or any record of his arrest in Chicago.

It had been disturbing enough that my insane ex had found me after all my precautions, but now it appeared he had never even been in jail, I was downright alarmed.

As I got back into Aunt Pandora's truck and headed toward Uncle Will's office, I thought back to Gil's attack on me, and what I'd been forced to do afterward to ensure my safety. My plan had seemed foolproof, but maybe the trauma of my psycho ex-boyfriend trying to murder me had impaired my reasoning.

Especially with Chief Neville claiming none of the past seventy-two hours had happened. Was it possible I was losing my mind?

No. There had to be some mistake, and when the chief checked with the Chicago police department again, they'd find it.

As I parked in front of Uncle Will's office and got out of the truck, I noticed Lucas Furman coming out of the diner. He tipped his Stetson at me but didn't meet my eyes. I watched as he got into a huge pickup and stared as he drove off.

Just a glimpse of him, and I felt on fire. My breath quickened, and my pulse raced. Either I was coming down with the flu, or the chemistry between us was that intense. At least for me. He hadn't seemed all that affected.

Shaking my head, I quickly went inside Uncle Will's building. I hoped he could explain everything from Elissa's fantasies to Chief Neville's claims, but in my heart of hearts, I was afraid the only explanation was one I wasn't ready to believe. Was it possible that magic really did exist?

CHAPTER NINE
Malice in Wonderland

As I entered the law offices, an extraordinarily beautiful man with white-blond hair sitting behind the desk glanced away from the computer. I had expected it to be just Uncle Will and me, but evidently, even attorneys conducted regular business on Sunday.

The receptionist's startling bright blue eyes examined me, then he cocked his head as if asking who I was and why I was there.

I introduced myself and waited for him to speak.

Instead, he quickly typed something and turned the screen so I could see it. HI! MY NAME IS EZEKIEL PROVO. I CAN'T HEAR OR SPEAK, BUT I CAN READ LIPS.

"Nice to meet you." Shaking his hand, I asked to see my uncle.

Ezekiel's fingers flew on the keyboard. MR. MAYER IS WITH A CLIENT BUT WILL BE FREE SHORTLY. HAVE A SEAT.

I nodded my thanks and sat on one of the two chairs flanking a coffee table. As I waited, I glanced at a magazine. It was one I didn't recognize but had some tasty sounding recipes and articles with interesting looking DIY projects.

Leafing through the pages, I tried to calm my racing thoughts, but they kept slipping back to Elissa's revelations and the police chief's odd behavior. I was lost in a fantasy of what my life might have been like if my father hadn't been murdered and he and my mother had raised me in Echo Springs, when an imposing woman with coal black hair swept by me and marched out the door.

She wore a gorgeous black and taupe Max Mara sheath with a pink linen blazer, shoes, and purse. I quickly added up the cost in my head, which came to a staggering thirty-five hundred dollars. And that didn't even count the jewelry.

"Calista, wait!" Uncle Will burst out of his office and scampered after the woman, but before he made it to the exit, I heard a car engine roar and tires squeal.

"I think you're too late," I murmured.

Turning to me, Uncle Will shrugged and said, "That didn't go as well as I'd hoped." He gestured for me to follow him and once we were behind his closed office door and he was sitting at his desk. He asked, "Did you sign the paperwork I gave you yesterday?"

"Not yet." I settled into the leather wing chair facing him. "I haven't had a chance to read them yet. I'll get to it tonight."

"Please do." Uncle Will's words were sharp, but he seemed to catch himself and added, "It's just imperative we tie up the loose ends so I can turn over the estate to you. I can allow you to live in Dora's house, but I can't grant you access to any funds without those documents completed."

"Sure. I understand." I frowned. "Does that mean I can't open up the candy store before the formalities are met?"

"No. You can open up." Uncle Will leaned forward. "In fact, it would be good if you went there for at least a few hours today. The keys are on the ring I gave you yesterday, and I'll call Inga Iverson and ask her to meet you there. She's worked for Pandora as long as I can remember and can get you going on the right path."

"Okey-dokey." I wondered why he was so eager for the store to be opened, but I had so many other questions I shoved that one aside and asked, "Who was that woman who stormed out of here?"

"Calista Pendergast, Cole's mother." Uncle Will's gaze fastened on a painting of Benjamin Franklin on the wall behind me. "She's been out of town, or you would have met her last night."

"Oh." I frowned. "She seemed sort of angry." I wasn't sure what it was about Calista that made me pursue the matter, but something was nudging me to find out what she was mad about.

"She was just upset that a matter she'd hoped would be resolved was still up in the air." Uncle Will continued to study Ben and his kite. "I can't say more. Attorney-client privilege, you understand."

"Right." I took a legal pad from my purse, clicked on my pen, and said, "I have a few questions."

"I'm sure you do." Uncle Will chuckled dryly.

"I'll start with the easy ones." I put a tick by the first item on my list. "Where can I buy a cell phone?"

Uncle Will's eyes twinkled as he opened a drawer in his desk, rummaged inside, and then tossed me a sealed box. I caught it and read the label. It was the newest version of the Samsung Android.

"I figured you'd need this." Uncle Will beamed. "It's on my plan now, but I'll set up a new account for you with Horizon. I'm afraid it's the only carrier that works in Echo Springs."

"Thank you," I stuttered. "You'll have to let me pay you for it."

"I'll add it to your legal bill." Uncle Will winked. "Which reminds me, I've also put you on my charge account. Here's a card you can use until we get the estate settled and you can set up your own line of credit."

"Wow. That is so sweet of you. Thanks again." I tucked the cell and credit card into my handbag, then asked, "Is there a real estate agent in town you can recommend?"

"Sorry. There isn't any." His knuckles whiten as he gripped

the edge of the desktop. "I hope you aren't thinking of selling Dora's house or the store."

"Not at the moment," I hedged. "But I can, right? It's not prohibited by her will?"

"Not in so many words." Uncle Will pursed his lips. "But I doubt you'd find any buyers. Outsiders are unaware of Echo Springs."

"Because the townspeople cast spells to keep Echo Springs hidden from outsiders?" I figured this was as perfect an opening as I would get to discuss Elissa's claims that we were all magical beings.

"Precisely." Uncle Will didn't blink at my outrageous statement. Instead, he seemed pleased that I'd brought it up.

"So..." I drew the word out unsure exactly how to proceed, then I mentally shrugged and blurted out, "Are telling me that everything Elissa claims is true?"

"If you're referring to the Ravenscraft Shield, the good and bad magic, and your powers, then yes," Uncle Will assured me.

Well crap! I sat there gaping at him as if he'd grown two heads. I had really been hoping he'd be the voice of reason.

When I remained silent he got up, walked around his desk, and sat in the chair beside me. "I know it's hard to believe, but that's why I was so worried about presenting you to the council at your welcome party." He took out a handkerchief and wiped his brow. "They insisted on meeting you immediately, and my magic isn't strong enough to resist their directives."

"Who are on the council?" Out of everything he'd just said, I'm not sure why I asked that particular question.

"Let's test your ability and see if you can name them." Uncle Will's nose twitched.

"Um." I thought back to last night, and immediately, faces started to pop into my head. "JFK, James Dean, Princess Diana, and that woman who reminded me of that country music singer. I couldn't think of her name."

"Right." Uncle Will beamed at me, "Patrick, Jeremy, Francine, and Virginia are four of the members. There are two more. You will be the seventh."

I concentrated then said, "Cole and Lucas."

"You got them all on your first try." Uncle Will chuckled. "Do you still doubt your ability?"

"You were afraid about introducing me to them before I was told about my power because one of them is the master or mistress of the corrupt magic," I guessed.

I was far from convinced, but it was hard to deny that as each image appeared in my head a sense of power radiated from all of them.

"Probably. Or one of their close family members." Uncle Will sighed. "I wasn't sure I'd be able to protect you and there was no time for Elissa to explain things to you beforehand or teach you to put up your own defenses."

"Why does most of the council look like dead celebrities?" Another random question that seemed to come out of my mouth instead of the more important ones. "I can't believe that's a coincidence. It really was Princess Di, JFK, James Dean, and..." I struggled to remember the singer's name.

"Patsy Cline," Uncle Will supplied. "And, yes it was them as they were known out in the world."

"I knew it." I pumped my fist.

Uncle Will shook his head at my immature display of enthusiasm and explained, "All citizens of Echo Springs are allowed to go out into the world for a certain period." He leaned back in his chair and seemed happy to teach me about the town.

"Like the Amish Rumspringa?"

"Pretty close. We call it Saorsa," He stroked his chin. "While the Amish leave their community in their teens, our people can go at any time. Most go in their twenties and return ten or fifteen years later."

"But why do they all seem to be the same age as when they died?"

"Within the confines of Echo Springs, we age as normal until we reach twenty-nine." Uncle Will tapped the arm of his chair. "After that, we grow older at a much slower rate. That's why most of those who choose to spend time in the outside world return before their thirty birthdays. When they're ready to return, they stage their deaths and come back."

"Princess Di was thirty-six, and JFK was well into his forties." I protested.

"Yes," Uncle Will tsked. "They got into a situation where it was difficult to make people believe they died." He shrugged. "And even though they waited for the right moment, there are still conspiracy theories about what happened to them."

"If they're born here," I knew that I needed to move on from this subject since I had so much more to talk about to Uncle Will, but I had to ask one more question, "how do they integrate into the outside world without just appearing out of nowhere?"

"One of our families has the ability to revise history. Cloe, one of the three sisters, can weave the backstory of the person entering the outside world into whatever situation they choose." He chuckled. "With social media so ubiquitous now, folks generally no longer choose the celebrity life as it's too difficult to return. Cloe can only reweave once per person so she can't do anything to help them with their exit."

"Then I'll stop aging at the normal rate too?" I still didn't believe everything, but this part sounded good.

Uncle Will nodded. "The only time you'll age at a normal rate is if you're outside of the Echo Springs city limits, which starts at the Ricochet Bridge."

"So you're..."

"A hundred and fifty-two." He smiled at my gasp.

While everything Uncle Will had related was fascinating, if not beyond bizarre, I decided it was time to move onto the matter of my dad. "What can you tell me about my father's murder?"

"It was one of the biggest losses Echo Springs has ever experienced." Uncle Will laced his fingers over his stomach and closed his eyes, then basically repeated what Elissa had already told me word for word.

"Didn't the police investigate?" I demanded. "Didn't they have any leads?"

"Chief Neville collected evidence, but there was nothing. No forensics. No witnesses. No security cameras." Uncle Will sighed. "Everyone assumed it was the master of the corrupt magic and knew that he or she would have removed all traces of their presence."

I thought about his explanation. Even if I believed the whole good versus bad magic scenario, whoever had deprived me of having a father and a family needed to be brought to justice. And with or without my alleged special abilities, I intended to find that person and make sure he or she was punished for taking my dad's life and ruining my mother's and mine.

CHAPTER TEN
Babe in the Woods

Uncle Will had contacted Inga Iverson, and she had agreed to meet me at six at the candy store to show me the ropes, which left me a little over an hour to grab something to eat. With Elissa's shocking claims, I hadn't been able to take more than a few bites of the lunch she'd provided, and my breakfast English muffin was long gone.

I considered going to the diner, but I wasn't ready to meet any more of Echo Springs' citizens. Which made me realize that I hadn't seen a single fast-food restaurant. No McDonald's. No Pizza Hut. No Starbucks. How would I survive?

After my initial panic, I could see the bright side. I'd save a heck of a lot of money, and doubtlessly, I'd also eat healthier— something I'd promised myself to do for quite a while. I'd start my new meal plan by going home and making myself a big salad.

Of course once I was back in Aunt Pandora's fabulous kitchen staring into the fully stocked refrigerator, I wavered and immediately rationalized that I'd hardly had anything all day, so I needed some protein. And dairy was part of the food pyramid. At least I thought it was.

Next thing I knew, I had built a thick ham and Swiss sandwich on a crusty baguette. I piled arugula and slices of pepper on top, then slathered the bread with Dijon mustard. After nabbing a Diet Coke and a container of deli potato salad from the fridge, I grabbed a fork and napkin, then wandered into the family room and flopped onto the couch.

Too tired to start digging through Aunt Pandora's desk, I picked up the remote and turned on the TV. With the weirdness

I'd already experienced in Echo Springs, I was half afraid the only channels would show reruns and old movies, but I was pleasantly surprised when I pushed the menu button and saw that my aunt had satellite. I was even happier to discover that she'd splurged on the deluxe package.

After a few minutes of watching various news programs, I clicked over to Bravo, which was showing a *Project Runway* marathon. Relaxing against the sofa's comfy cushions, I bit into my sandwich and watched Tim Gunn tell the contestants to "make it work."

By the time I was full, and they had sent the loser to pack up his scissors, it was five-fifty-seven. Leaping from the sofa, I brushed the crumbs from my shirt, ran out to the truck, and jumped behind the wheel.

Thank goodness, the house was only a couple streets over from the candy store. I made it to the shop a socially acceptable five minutes behind schedule.

The door swung open before I reached it and a slender ash blonde in her fifties said with a slight Swedish accent, "You are late."

"Sorry." I automatically apologized, but then I recalled that I was her boss and said, "I can't wait to see *my* store. Thank you for meeting me on such short notice."

"It is good you are here." Inga moved aside, and I stepped over the threshold.

"Hmm," I murmured noncommittally. The verdict was still out on that point.

She led me through a maze of antique tables that held a variety of gift items and other bric-a-brac, past a candy display case, and to the register. Surprisingly, it was a modern computerized version, not the vintage brass one I'd been expecting.

"Pandora and I alternated days." Inga reached under the

counter for a notebook, flipped it open, and handed it to me. "Usually we are open from ten to six, but because we have been closed for so long, I felt tonight could be an exception."

A quick glance showed that my aunt worked Tuesday, Thursday, Friday, and Sunday, while Inga had Monday, Wednesday, and Saturday. It seemed like a breeze after my long hours and six-day weeks at Crystal's Closet.

"So the shop doesn't get busy enough to warrant more than one clerk at a time?"

It concerned me a little that the store might not make enough money to live on. I still wasn't sure what kind of estate my aunt had left me. I really needed to read those papers Uncle Will had given me to sign.

"It is more a steady stream of customers than a huge rush at one time." Inga's expression was stolid. "But do not worry. We keep busy."

"Well, that's good." I studied the small shop. "I've worked retail before, and I know getting slammed isn't fun. People can be so impatient."

Inga nodded, but didn't comment, instead, she asked, "Shall I give you a tour and show you the books?"

"That would be great."

She guided me through an archway at the rear of the store and opened a door. "We have three rooms back here. This is the largest, and we rent it out for meetings and to the bakery when they host a ladies' high tea."

It was furnished with several round tables and chairs and decorated in vintage wallpaper. The light fixtures all had rose-colored glass that cast a flattering glow on anyone seated below them.

"The next largest is our prep area. Your aunt used it to concoct our signature truffles." Inga opened the door, and I saw a stainless steel counter, refrigerator, and cooktop. "Once she perfected the recipe, I would take over and make them in bulk."

"I'd like to attempt to continue that practice." I had tried my hand at some candy making last Christmas and given my best customers small boxes of my chocolates as gifts. They'd been a big hit.

"Certainly." Inga led me to the last door in the hallway and opened it. "This is our storage room." She gestured to the shelving that took up the left side, then pointed to a large floor safe and a tiny desk on the right. "Pandora used this as an office as well."

Inga walked inside the room, opened a drawer, and handed me a thumb drive. "The combination to the safe is on this, as is the store's accounts." She stared at me, appraisingly. "I hope you know Quick Books."

"Nope." I shrugged and crossed my fingers. "But I'm a fast learner." Which was the truth, unless my notoriously bad math skills turned out to be a problem.

As Inga and I returned to the front of the store, a middle-aged man dressed in worn jeans, a chambray shirt, and a faded green John Deere gimme cap thrust open the glass door and walked inside.

He scanned the shop and his gaze immediately fastened on me. He nodded, apparently to himself, took off his hat, and moved until he and I were too close for my comfort. Then without uttering a word, he proceeded to gawk at me.

When I stepped back from him and quickly darted behind the candy counter, he cleared his throat and announced, "I'm Ray Halsey. Lucas Furman told me you were finally here."

Having swooned at Lucas's feet upon meeting him, I wondered exactly what the smoking hot rancher had said about me. Faylynn had already mentioned that her cousin had told her about me, and now apparently, Lucas had talked about me to this guy too.

My fainting like a damsel in distress was a less-than-flattering moment I was trying hard to forget. I could only hope that Lucas wasn't telling that story all over town.

Instead of asking Mr. Halsey what Lucas had shared about our encounter, which is what I truly wanted to know, I pasted on my professional saleswoman smile and said, "Welcome to Pandora's."

The man ignored my greeting and marched toward the display case that I'd put between us as if he were on a mission from the president. Or maybe someone even more important like Oprah.

Coming to an abrupt stop in front of a tray of mocha truffles, he announced, "You're just in time."

For what? I knew some people were chocoholics, but this seemed a bit of an overreaction.

Covering my confusion, I kept my expression pleasant as I asked, "Would you like a sample?"

"No." The guy's brown eyes flashed with annoyance. "I want you to do something about Oscar."

"Oscar?"

"He's dying."

"That's terrible." I glanced to where Inga had been standing, but she'd disappeared. "Have you taken him to the hospital?"

Mr. Halsey gave me a strange look and said, "How would I take a tree to the hospital?"

"A tree?" Thank goodness. I mean, it's sad if a tree dies, but at least it wasn't a person. "Your tree is dying, and you're looking for someone to save it?"

"Yes."

"Oh." So what the heck was he doing in a candy store?

We were both silent, staring at each other, then he said, "He protects my farm and makes my crops grow."

"Your tree?"

Was everyone in this town nuts? Taking into consideration the Echo Springians that I'd met so far, my vote was a resounding yes.

"Uh, huh."

I still had no clue as to why he was telling me all this, but never one to mind my own business, I suggested, "Then you need a…" I paused, thinking, "… a tree doctor. They have those, don't they?"

"What the hell are you talking about?" Mr. Halsey's ruddy complexion turned an angry purple. "It's your job to save Oscar, not some gardener."

"What are *you* talking about? My job is to sell candy." Hoping to get rid of the lunatic, I snatched a chocolate from the display case and thrust it at him. "Here. What you need is a sample."

"Okay. If that's what I need." He plucked the truffle from the paper cup. "Should I bury it by his trunk or apply it to his bark?"

Shit! "Neither." What was up with this guy? "You're supposed to eat it."

Mr. Halsey shrugged, then with a hopeful expression on his face, he popped it into his mouth. Chewing, he asked, "Is that it?"

"Uh. I guess so." Then remembering my retail training, I added, "Unless you'd like to make a purchase."

He snarled something I didn't catch and reached across the counter. As his fingers closed over my wrist, an odd, tilting feeling swept over me—almost like motion sickness. The air seemed to become syrupy, and it was if I'd inhaled a trace of chloroform.

I must have looked like I was going to faint or throw up because Mr. Halsey let go of me and jumped back.

This time his tone was more respectful, almost pleading. "Just tell me what to do, whatever the cost. I'll do it. I can't lose my farm."

My wrist still tingled where he had touched me, and I absently rubbed the area with my other hand. Immediately the sensation came over me again, only this time it was much stronger. I felt like I wasn't solid anymore, almost as if the 'me' in me was fading away.

My eyes were drawn to the white paper candy cup I still held in my palm. There was writing on the bottom, and I squinted to read it. Listen to the Earth's heartbeat and dance.

Mr. Halsey was now muttering to himself, and when he reached into his pocket, I was afraid he had a gun, so I hurriedly shoved the wrapper at him. "Look. There's something printed here." Trying to distract him, I babbled, "It's like a fortune cookie."

He glanced down, then scowled at me. "What are you jabbering about? There's nothing written there."

I checked the cup. The words were still there. Why didn't he see them? Was this further evidence that he was crazy or was I the one who was insane?

Elissa's voice popped into my head, "The candy store has been the conduit by which we provide our assistance. We investigate the complaint, decide what's required, and give out what's needed."

Suddenly a kink in my mind seemed to smooth out. I stepped from behind the counter and walked directly to a small table near the entrance. Both the man and Inga, who had reappeared as mysteriously as she'd vanished, followed me. Unhesitatingly, I reached for an exquisitely carved wooden music box and handed it to Mr. Halsey.

He cradled it to his chest, a look of peace on his face.

Inga prodded me, "Tell him what to do."

I immediately said, "Listen to the Earth's heartbeat and dance."

He nodded his expression content. "What do I owe you?"

"A favor to be named later." Had that come out of my mouth?

Mr. Halsey nodded again, scribbled an IOU on the back of a feed bill, and said, "I'll let you know what happens."

"You do that." I steered him toward the exit, wanting to get rid of him so I could think about what had just happened. "Bye."

As I held the door open for him to leave. I noticed Cole Pendergast standing across the street. His expression was unreadable until his intense blue eyes locked onto mine and sent my pulse racing.

I knew I was staring like a lovesick jack-o'-lantern, but I couldn't make myself stop. The heat of his gaze swept over me like a tsunami. For the first time, I truly understood the meaning of the words "animal magnetism" and I fought a desperate urge to cross the road and throw myself into his arms.

The look on his face said he was having similar thoughts. Then suddenly he flashed me a sexy smile, waved, and walked away. A heartbeat later, I realized I had been holding my breath and exhaled. The return of oxygen to my system kick-started my brain. I quickly stepped back inside and firmly closed the door behind.

I turned, looking around for Inga to ask her what had just happened with the candy and the music box, but she had disappeared again. We needed to have a little talk about that habit of hers. I figured she had returned to the back room, but when I walked back there, it was empty. Somewhat bewildered, but strangely at peace as if I had just finished reading a book with a really satisfying ending, I sank into the desk chair.

My life had become a revolving door that spits people at me at random times. And evidently, I was supposed to know what to do with those individuals. But how could I figure out which ones to trust, which ones to help, and which ones to guard against?

Leaning back in my seat, I mulled over the possibility that magic might truly exist and that I possessed it.

CHAPTER ELEVEN
Used Karma

The next morning, I just couldn't make myself get out of bed. I had a million things to do, but sitting up seemed to be a herculean task that was beyond me.

After falling back asleep the third or fourth time, it occurred to me that I might be in some kind of shock. In the past week, I'd discovered that I wasn't who I thought I was, my ex had tried to kill me, not once, but twice, and those two little events weren't even the most astounding item on my list of what had happened to me.

Despite a mighty struggle not to accept it, I was beginning to think what Elissa had told me might be true. I could really be the Ravenscraft Shield, and it was possible that I wielded magical power. Which apparently was the norm for my new hometown.

Pulling the blanket over my head, I snuggled into Aunt Pandora's super comfortable mattress. If I was sleeping, I could pretend that it all was just a dream.

Finally, the need to pee forced me out of bed. Then once I was up and awake, my stomach rumbled loud enough to wake the dead, which considering what I'd been told about Echo Springs was not something I wanted to chance happening. I absolutely refused to see if ghosts were included among the town's magical citizens.

After taking care of my most pressing need, I showered, then threw on a pair of yoga pants and a long-sleeved T-shirt. It might be spring, but I still felt cold.

It was Inga's day to work at the candy shop and I wasn't

planning to leave the house, so I let my hair dry naturally and didn't bother with makeup. Normally I straightened my curls and never appear in public without my blush and mascara, but once in a while, it was nice not to mess with any styling products or cosmetics.

While I ate my usual breakfast, I pulled out my trusty legal pad and made a list of what I had to do. Reading the estate papers from Uncle Will should have been number one, but every time I picked them up, the tiny print seemed to blur, and I got a headache. Maybe I needed to have my eyes examined for glasses.

Vowing to go through the pages tonight, I looked over the rest of my tasks.

1. GO THROUGH AUNT PANDORA'S DESK AND FILE CABINET.

2. EXAMINE THE CANDY SHOP'S BOOKS.

3. EXPLORE THE REST OF THE HOUSE.

Shoot! I had forgotten to ask Uncle Will about the keys to the locked rooms.

I started to reach into the front pocket of my yoga pants for my cell phone, then stopped. He'd ask about the estate papers, and I was embarrassed to admit they were strewn across the floor in the family room. I'd flung them there after my second or third attempt to make sense out of one of the paragraphs on the first page.

I brightened. Maybe the missing keys were in Pandora's desk, and I wouldn't have to bother my honorary uncle. Or I could always wait another day to tackle the second and third floors.

Draining the last drop of coffee, I placed my mug in the sink, dusted the English muffin crumbs from my chest, and strolled into the family room. Pandora's office chair was leather, and I sighed as I sank into the cushiony seat. My aunt definitely knew how to treat herself.

The desk had three drawers, and the top one held a stack of scratch pads—the type charities mailed out hoping to guilt the recipients into donating—, a three pack of scotch tape, a glue stick, a large box of various colored paperclips, and a calculator bearing the logo of the Echo Springs bank.

The middle drawer was empty except for a bottle of Remy Martin and two crystal glasses. Did Aunt Pandora regularly share her expensive cognac or was the second glass there for an occasional visitor? I wished that I'd had the chance to meet her.

It was beyond annoying that when I tried to pull out the third drawer, it wouldn't budge. Another key I needed to locate. Or I could always find a screwdriver and force it open.

But before doing anything drastic, I'd go through the mounds of paper that covered every square inch of the desktop. When I pawed through the piles of bills, junk mail, and magazines, I noticed that a lot had dates going back several months and it dawned on me I didn't know the cause of Pandora's death. Had she been sick or was it something sudden like a fall from a ladder?

Another question I'd have to add to the ones already buzzing around in my head. I probably need to make a list of those to add to all the other lists currently on the sheets of my legal pad.

Blowing out a long put-upon sigh, I leaned back and closed my eyes. Before I could take refuge in sleep again, there was a throbbing near my crotch. Either my new cell phone was set to vibrate, or something weird was going on with my body. In view of everything I'd been through, I give even odds for either possibility.

The phone was still pulsing, and it was starting to feel a little too good, so I dug it out of my pocket, thumbed the icon, and said, "Hello."

I was expecting Uncle Will to be on the other end of the line since I hadn't given this number to anyone else, but instead, an attractive baritone asked, "Alexandria?"

"Yes." The voice sounded familiar, but I couldn't place it.

"This is Lucas Furman. We met briefly at your welcome party."

"Of course." I mean really, how could I forget fainting at the man's feet? "Please call me Lexie."

"You do seem more like a Lexie." There was a pause, then he said, "I was wondering if you were free for dinner sometime this week."

"I...uh," I stuttered. "It's very nice of you to ask, but..."

If what Elissa had told me was true, it probably wasn't a good idea to be alone with any of Echo Springs' citizens. And even if she was a raving lunatic, after my ex's behavior, dating was not anywhere on my radar. Then there was the whole we should kill her conversation I'd heard or imagined when I passed out.

"Before you say no," Lucas interrupted my thoughts. "Would you feel more comfortable if my dad came along? He wasn't feeling well the day of the party and would like to meet you."

"Well..." I wasn't sure why I didn't just say no, which would have been the smart move.

"My father and yours were friends, and he thought you might like to hear some of his memories of Nathanial," Lucas interjected smoothly.

"Oh." That put a different spin on things. I definitely wanted to learn more about my dad. "That would be great. How about Wednesday?"

"Terrific," Lucas agreed. "Would the diner be okay?" He chuckled. "The only nice restaurant in town is owned by the Pendergasts and Pop isn't too fond of supporting their business."

"Absolutely." No one had mentioned a feud between the Furmans and the Pendergasts. Another question for my list. "What time should we meet there?"

"Does six sound good? I'd be happy to pick you up at home," Lucas offered. "Parking can get a little tight near the diner during the supper rush."

"Six is fine, but there isn't any need to come here." No way was I getting into a car with anyone until I figured out if someone truly wanted me dead or if I had been hallucinating when I heard that threat. "I can use the spot behind the candy store and walk over."

"Sure. I'll see you Wednesday then." Lucas said goodbye and hung up.

Deep in thought, I returned to sorting through the mess on the desktop. I had just tossed away the last of the junk mail and was getting the bills in chronological order when my phone vibrated again.

This time I checked the display before answering and saw it was Cole Pendergast. I debated letting the call go to voicemail but shrugged and picked up. It wouldn't hurt to talk to him.

"Hello."

"Alexandria, this is Cole."

Hmm. Interesting that unlike Lucas, he didn't seem to feel the need to remind me how we'd met.

"Did you get my number from Will?" I'd forgotten to ask Lucas about that.

"I did." His smooth tenor deepened. "I hope you don't mind."

"I'm just surprised that he'd share it without asking me first."

"Well..." Cole's voice seemed a lot less assured than before. "Anyway, I was hoping you'd agree to have dinner with me."

"I'm afraid that with settling in and working at the candy

store, I don't have time." I had the same reservations about being alone with him that I had about being alone with Lucas.

"Would you be more comfortable if my mother joined us? She'd like to meet you."

"I see." He and Lucas seemed to think along the same lines, and I silently chuckled, wondering if they realized that. Or maybe they compared notes. Just because their parents didn't like each other didn't mean they weren't friends.

"Mother was so sorry to have missed your welcome party," Cole added when I didn't elaborate.

Judging from Mrs. Prendergast's rude behavior at Uncle Will's office, I wasn't sure I wanted to meet her. Still, she was around the right age, so she might have information about my father.

"How sweet of her," I kept my tone neutral. "How does Saturday work for you and your mom? We could have brunch? Say one o'clock,"

"That would be fine," Cole agreed. "We can dine in the private room at my restaurant. We have a world-renowned chef, so I'd love to give him carte blanche for the menu. Do you have any food allergies?"

"Nope." I glanced at the time and said, "Then I'll see you Saturday at one. Bye." I quickly hung up and dialed Uncle Will.

He picked up on the first ring and after we dealt with the pleasantries, he said, "Did you get those papers signed? If so, I can pick them up on my way home tonight."

"Sorry. No." My cheeks warmed. He'd been so nice, and I hated to let him down so I joked, "The legalese keeps giving me a headache."

"We could make an appointment and I could go over them with you," he offered.

"Thank you, but I won't waste your time like that. I'll for sure get them signed by tomorrow morning." I had a graduate degree; surely, I could comprehend some estate documents. "However, I do have a few questions you might be able to answer."

"Whatever I can do to help," he quickly said. "Just name it."

"Great. Where are the keys to the upstairs rooms and Pandora's desk?"

"Let me think." Uncle Will was silent then said, "I'm not sure where the original sets are, but I believe Dora kept spares in the freezer. The package should be marked 'liver'. She hated that stuff and thought most other people did as well." He chuckled. "Anything else?"

"Yes." I nodded although he couldn't see me. "There are a lot of overdue bills among the mail on top of her desk. How should I handle them?"

"As executor, I can pay them. Drop them at my office tomorrow when you bring the estate documents by."

Right. I had just promised to have those papers signed by then, hadn't I?

Hastily changing the subject, I said, "That reminds me, what was the cause of Aunt Pandora's death?"

"The chimney for the fireplace malfunctioned," Uncle Will sniffled. "She died of carbon monoxide poisoning."

"Oh, my gosh! How did that happen?"

"I'm not sure of all the details, but as it was explained to me, it had something to do with soot buildup and the age of the flue liner." He sighed. "Dora had just had new windows and insulation installed, and it worked a little too well. The airtight seal caused a fatal accumulation of CO in the house."

"That's awful." I glanced at the fireplace. I would definitely not be using it if I was still around come winter.

"I hate to cut you off, but I have a client waiting. Was there anything else?"

"Both Cole and Lucas called." I tried not to sound accusing, but I had to ask, "Did you give my number to anyone else?"

"Just the council members," Uncle Will said. "I hope you don't mind."

"No. I understand." What else could I say? "But please don't share it again without asking me."

"No. Sorry." He cleared his throat. "Call me if you need anything. Bye."

After I disconnected, I located the desk and room keys in the freezer, but I was too restless to use them. Instead, I decided to go for a drive. I wanted to see how far Echo Springs reached in all directions.

Just in case the whole aging thing was real, I wasn't planning on leaving the city limits. I was too close to thirty to chance it.

I didn't bother to change clothes or put on makeup. Instead, I twisted my hair into a messy bun on top of my head, perched a large pair of sunglasses on my nose, and walked out to the garage. I wasn't planning to get out of the truck, and anyone seeing me through the windshield wouldn't be able to tell that I was less than my usual put-together self.

The Echo Springs phone book I'd found in the kitchen junk drawer might have been the thinnest one I'd ever seen, but its first page had been a map of the town. Figuring I would need it many times in the future, I'd torn it out and now laid it on the passenger seat where I could quickly glance at it as I drove.

Uncle Will had driven me into the downtown area from the east, so I headed west. This direction was as rural as the one we'd traveled through, and leaving the reassuring trappings of civilization made me shiver.

Having been a city girl most of my life, the endless fields were nerve-wracking. From what little I remembered learning in school about Kansas, I knew that it had been scraped flat eons ago by massive glaciers. And today the wind was taking full advantage of the level surface to make the trees and wheat stalks bow to its superiority.

It hadn't been as blustery in town and I fought to keep the truck from weaving back and forth. Once I turned on a gravel road it was even worse, especially with the washboard ruts, and I almost couldn't stop when the road abruptly ended at a closed gate with a huge tree beside it.

There hadn't been another vehicle on the road or another soul in sight since I left town and all this openness was giving me the willies.

Just as I'd put the truck in reverse, I caught someone waving at me as he hurriedly pushed open the gate and ran toward me. My inclination was to get the heck out of there, but then I recognized the man from the candy store and my curiosity won over my common sense.

I rolled down the window and Mr. Halsey rushed over. He was a changed man. The smile on his face erased several years from my original estimate of his age, and his eyes twinkled warmly as he grasped my hand.

"It worked!" He pumped my hand up and down. "Oscar is cured."

"That's terrific." I had no idea what to think. Had I really cured his tree? "Here, see what he was like yesterday." He held out his phone and showed me a photo of a tree that looked as if it was ready to be cut down for firewood. Then he jerked his thumb over his shoulder at the maple I'd noticed by the gate. "Look at Oscar now."

"That can't be the same tree." I wondered why Mr. Halsey was trying to fool me.

"Check out the date and the details on the picture." He thrust the phone into my hand.

I studied the image. The date was a couple of days ago, and the rest of the snapshot matched what was before my eyes. My throat tight, I nodded my acceptance.

"Anything you need, I'm your man." Mr. Halsey beamed. "I've got your back."

I thanked him, turned the truck around, and headed back to town. Why did I feel so lost? Was it because I was suddenly forced to look for pieces of myself that I didn't even know had been missing?

CHAPTER TWELVE
Just for the Spell of It

I woke up Tuesday morning still trying to convince myself that Echo Springs and all its citizens were crazy to believe in magic. But the minute I thought about leaving town before something even weirder happened to me, an image of Oscar flitted through my mind.

Just the fact that I was calling a tree by name should have made me hightail it back to Chicago, but then the two pictures of the maple popped into my head. They were identical, right down to the rust spot on the metal gate and the vine growing out of the top of the pipe that acted as a side post.

Either Mr. Halsey was quite the expert with Photoshop or Oscar had really been at death's door before I gave his owner the music box.

As I showered and got ready to go to the candy store, I had to admit that I was beginning to believe everything Elissa had told me. That meant either I was as nutso as everyone else or there really was magic in the world.

While I ate breakfast, I glanced guiltily at the stack of papers next to my plate. I'd only gotten through two or three pages before the print began to swim again. Maybe I should just trust Uncle Will and sign them.

Shaking my head, I decided to pick up a pair of reading glasses somewhere after work and give it one more try before admitting defeat. I was relieved that Uncle Will wasn't at his law office when I dropped off the bundle of Aunt Pandora's bills. If he'd been there, I'd have to admit to him I hadn't completed the papers yet.

Inga had told me about the tiny parking area in back of the candy store and said I should use it instead of taking up prime space in front of the shop. I easily found the alley leading to the private lot and pulled the truck into one of the three empty slots.

Grabbing my purse, I slid out from behind the wheel. I was checking to make sure I had my phone as I crossed the gravel toward the back of the store when the roar of an engine made me look up.

My heart stopped as I stared at a huge black cargo van barreling toward me. The situation brought back the memory of my ex trying to run me over at the bridge and thankfully my reflexes didn't wait for my mind to catch up because without thinking about it, I raced toward the metal dumpster and cowered behind it.

The van hesitated as if considering another try at me, but when the rear door of the shop was flung open, it squealed its tires and took off. Inga glanced after the fleeing vehicle, then scanned the area until she spotted me still crouched behind the garbage bin.

Without a ripple marring her smooth forehead, Inga asked, "Are you coming inside?"

I nodded and hurriedly followed her through the door, making sure I locked it behind me. My throat convulsed as I tried to swallow my fear and speak, but the adrenaline pumping through my veins made it impossible to force any words from between my trembling lips.

Finally, I was able to take a deep breath and said, "We should call the police. That van deliberately tried to run me over."

"What will they do?" Inga asked. "Did you get the license plate?"

"No." I mentally slapped my forehead. Why hadn't I done that? "But how many black cargo vans can there be in a town this size."

"Telephone Chief Neville if you wish, but whoever was driving that van didn't own it. If I were going to use a vehicle to commit a homicide, I'd steal it from somewhere outside of Echo Springs and return it before the owner even noticed it was missing."

Instead of calming me down, the fact that Inga came up with a plan like that so quickly scared the crap out of me. Could she be in on the scheme to kill me? Wait a minute. Why was she even here? And how had she known to open the backdoor at that exact time?

Pinning her with a stare, I said, "Isn't it my day to work?"

"Yes." Inga pointed to the dress she wore. "I just dropped by on my way to bible study to see if you had any questions before your first shift."

"Oh. That was nice of you. Thanks." Okay. I'd give her that. "What made you come out to the alley? Did you hear the engine?"

She pointed to a garbage bag near her feet. "I forgot to put this in the trash yesterday before I left and I wanted to make sure you had a clean start."

"Well, thanks again." A reasonable answer, but I was still suspicious. I shooed her out of the shop and said, "I'll be fine. Enjoy your day off."

As soon as she left, I locked the door behind her, dug through my purse, and found the card Chief Neville had given me at the welcome party. Opening my cell phone to the contacts, I was about to put in the chief's number when I saw that Uncle Will had thoughtfully added the names and numbers of everyone on the council, as well as the chief's information.

But how had he managed that? I was sure the package the cell phone had come in was sealed. Maybe since it was on his plan, he had remote access. And if that were the case, I needed to switch to my own plan ASAP.

But before I dealt with that issue, I needed to talk to the police. As Inga had predicted, the chief was less than impressed with my report.

"Ms. Ravenscraft, you are beginning to sound a bit paranoid." Chief Neville chuckled. "First, your ex tries to kill you by running you off the road, now someone else comes at you in a black van."

"Maybe Gil didn't die in the river, and it's him back for another try."

"Or it was just a bunch of kids out for a joy ride," Chief Neville said, his tone expressing his lack of interest.

"But it's a school day," I blurted out.

"Those types of kids didn't exactly mind playing hooky." The chief didn't bother to hide his exasperation. "Relax. No one is out to get you."

That wasn't what Elissa had told me. But she had mentioned that Chief Neville wasn't one who embraced his magic so maybe he didn't believe all that good versus evil stuff that my cousin had spouted.

The chief grudgingly took my report, but I could tell he wouldn't do anything about my near miss. It was especially evident when I asked if he was sending someone out to look at the crime scene.

"Don't be ridiculous." Chief Neville laugh was dismissive. "What is there to see? This mysterious van didn't hit anything, right?"

"No. But how about tread marks or something like that?" I suggested.

"Goodbye Ms. Ravenscraft." He disconnected, and I stared at my phone.

That had not gone well at all.

Sighing, I returned to the storeroom and tucked my purse

away in the desk drawer. Then I picked up one of the red-and-white striped aprons stacked on the shelves and tied it around my waist.

I had a price list of our merchandise, I knew how to run the register, and I was ready for my first shift. Or at least as prepared as possible.

After I unlocked the door and flipped the sign to open, I wandered through the aisles familiarizing myself with the merchandise. I had already studied the list of candy, but the rest of our stock seemed to be one of a kind items. There were marble eggs, goblets, fancy mirrors, bells, and various perfume bottles.

I was inspecting a tiny vial hanging from an intricate silver chain, when a young woman limped into the shop. She grimaced with every step she took, and her expression reflected the agony she felt as she moved toward me.

Examining her face, I could see the deep grooves carved around her mouth. Immediately, I knew that this was a person in chronic pain and that she had lived with that pain for quite some time. I could tell that it was the type of misery that would incapacitate most people, but the woman gritted her teeth and didn't stop until she was in front of me.

"Alexandria Ravenscraft?" Her voice was sweet, and she held out a slim hand.

"Yes." I shook her hand, noting the chill in her thin white fingers. The same odd tilting feeling I'd experienced with Mr. Halsey swept over me. My head swam, and I had to fight to remain standing. I forced back the nausea and asked, "May I help you?"

Call me crazy, but I was guessing she hadn't stopped by to buy a bag of licorice.

"My name is Harmony Triton, and as you may have noticed, I have mobility issues."

Unsure how to respond, which seemed to happen a lot since I arrived in Echo Springs, I nodded and then hazarded a guess, "Arthritis?"

"Sirenomelia." I must have looked confused because she explained, "Mermaid Syndrome. My legs were fused together at birth. I underwent several surgeries to separate them, but walking is excruciating, and the doctors could do little for the pain."

"I'm so sorry." Maybe she had stopped by for candy. I'd need a lot of chocolate to get through the day if I was in constant torment.

"Sadly, your aunt wasn't able to help, but she assured me that once the new Shield arrived, you would be able to cure me."

"I'll certainly try, but I'm new at all this." I wanted to take away this brave young woman's pain, but I had no idea how to do it.

"Well." Her lips quirked into a half smile. "It's not like I have anything to lose."

"Okay. Give me a second." What were the steps I'd taken with Mr. Halsey?

Ah. Yes. I rubbed the area that tingled where he had touched me.

Bracing myself, I brought my hands together as if in prayer. Immediately I lost the sense of being solid and felt like I was experiencing the world around me from another dimension.

My eyes were drawn to the candy case where a greenish glow surrounded a mint truffle. I walked unsteadily behind the counter and took it out.

Extending the chocolate delicacy to Harmony, I breathed, "Eat this."

Once she popped the truffle into her mouth, chewed, and swallowed, I stared at the white paper candy cup remaining in my palm. There was writing on the bottom that read: DARE TO

LOVE COMPLETELY.

Lifting my gaze to Harmony, I asked, "Are you seeing someone?"

She glanced away, red coloring her milk-white cheeks. "I don't date."

"Why is that?" I couldn't believe I was asking a relative stranger such a personal question, but something inside compelled me to continue.

Harmony gestured to her legs. "Because it wouldn't be fair to saddle someone with this."

"But you have feelings for someone, right?" I persisted, all the time wondering when she would tell me to mind my own business.

"Yes," Harmony said so softly I nearly didn't hear her response.

"And does he have feelings for you?" *Geesh!* Could I get more personal?

"Eric's asked me out, but I've always said no." Harmony's blush deepened. "He still walks me home after choir practice every Wednesday and hangs around my shop even when he doesn't need a haircut." Her aqua eyes shined when she whispered. "He brings me lunch nearly every day. He only misses if he needs to take care of police business."

"So Eric is a police officer?" I asked, then recalling that I'd given Mr. Halsey a music box to complete the charm, I studied the various tables of merchandise scattered through the shop.

"Uh-huh. His name is Eric Barnes." Harmony answered. "Have you met him?"

"No." I concentrated harder, and finally, an object called to me.

I walked over to a table full of jewelry and spotted a shell with a pearl peeking out of its tiny opening. It was hanging from a delicate gold chain, and I picked it up, then returned to

Harmony and held it out to her.

She eagerly began to fasten it around her neck, but I put my hand over her fingers and said, "Wear this and dare to love completely."

"You mean Eric?" Her inability to credit her good fortune shone in her eyes.

"Yes. Tell him how you feel and let him tell you how he feels."

"But my legs..." Harmony stuttered. "He's so handsome. He should have someone perfect."

"Someone perfect for him is much more important than physical perfection." I had learned that lesson the hard way with Gil. "And if the charm works, who knows what will happen." I raised my brows. "Put on the necklace."

Harmony slipped the chain over her head and blinked. "I... I think some of the pain is fading."

"Well, that's great news." I smiled widely. "Now go find your Eric."

I could sense the relief coming off of Harmony as she walked toward the door.

When she paused, my heart dropped, but then she said, "How much do I owe you?"

"You mentioned your shop. Are you a hair stylist?" When she nodded, I gingerly touched my hair. "Can you get this back to my original color and fix the hatchet job I did on it when I tried to cut it myself?"

"Definitely." Harmony beamed. "Stop by after you close the Candy Box. My place is right next to the bookstore."

"Then we'll call it even."

After Harmony left, I found myself humming. If I could help people like her, maybe being the Shield wouldn't be so bad.

CHAPTER THIRTEEN
Sense and Sense Ability

The rest of my shift at Pandora's Candy Box was uneventful. As Inga promised, there was a steady stream of customers, but never more than two or three people in line at any one time. The townspeople all mentioned how pleased they were to have the shop open again and seemed genuinely happy to welcome me to their community.

After I closed up at six and put the cash drawer in the safe, I left my car in the parking lot and walked over to Beyond the Mirror. Harmony finished with the woman in her chair, sent her off to pay at the front counter, and waved me over to the shampoo sinks.

Before my butt touched the seat, she said, "I have a date with Eric tonight."

"Terrific." I was impressed that she'd moved so fast. But I guess knife-like pain every time she took a step was pretty motivating.

"And, my legs are about fifty percent better." Harmony walked back and forth in front of me to demonstrate her new mobility.

"That's amazing." I smiled, then frowned as a new thought occurred to me. "How did you manage to be on your feet all day here in your shop?"

"I used a stool when it got too bad." She grimaced, then brightened and said, "But enough about that. Describe your original color to me."

"Sort of an apricot copper." I wish I had pictures to show her. Too bad they'd all been on my phone—the one I'd destroyed and left in Chicago to prevent Gil from tracking me down. "But anything close to that is fine."

"Hmm." Harmony nodded thoughtfully as she ran her fingers through my hair. "I can do that. And how short are you willing to go?"

"I'd like to keep as much length as possible." I hated the whine in my voice, but I'd always had long hair, and it had been traumatic losing the six inches I'd cut for my disguise.

"With your natural curl, unless you want to have to straighten it every day, it would be best to go with a side part and layers."

"Sounds good." I sat back and hoped Harmony's magical ability was fixing hair disasters.

Ninety minutes later, feeling happier about my appearance than I had since I'd arrived in Echo Springs, I walked to my truck and headed home. Harmony had done a remarkable job, and I kept glancing in the pickup's rearview mirror to admire my restored color and new cut.

Once I'd eaten supper, I was too tired to do much besides watch television, and I went to bed as soon as the ten o'clock news was over.

I spent most of the next day learning the store's bookkeeping system and looking through Aunt Pandora's computer files. I was hoping for one marked Shield or magic or ability or even instructions, but all I found were cute cat pictures and lots of recipes.

When I wasn't working, I obsessed about the black van that had tried to run me over. It had taken all the nerve I could summon to return to the candy store's lot and retrieve the truck after my hair appointment, and I wasn't looking forward to having to face that again this evening when I parked there to meet Lucas and his father at the diner.

At four thirty, I headed into the shower. I intended to look my best for this dinner. Lucas had seen me at my worst and I wanted to replace that picture of me in his mind with a better image.

Although I wasn't ready to date or even feel safe around him right now, if the whole someone-wants-to-kill-me-good-versus-evil-ex-boyfriend-trauma ever was resolved, I wanted Lucas to be interested in asking me out. I mean come on, he was one of the hottest men that I'd ever seen.

It took me nearly forty-five minutes to get my makeup and hair just right. Then another quarter-hour to find just the perfect outfit. I finally chose a pair of dark wash fitted jeans with an apricot T-shirt and navy jacket. Some gold hoop earrings, an infinity scarf, and black mid-heeled ankle boots pulled the ensemble together.

It was five forty when I parked in back of the candy store and after a quick check that no mysterious black vans were idling anywhere in sight, I bolted out of the truck and ran until I was safely on Main Street. I slowed as I approached the Wizard of Hogs, and by the time I pushed open the diner's door, I was able to stroll inside as if I didn't have a care in the world.

A middle-aged man who barely reached my chin was standing by the register. When he saw me, he darted from behind the counter and nearly bowed.

Beaming, he said, "Ms. Ravenscraft, you honor us with your presence." His resemblance to a bandy rooster was increased when he stuck out his chin and said, "I am Ambrose Hoggs, your humble host."

His front teeth mesmerized me. They stuck out like a pair of light switches at half-mast. I'd never seen that particular dental oddity before, and growing up on the wrong side of the trailer courts and apartments, I'd seen a lot of bad orthodontia.

It took me a moment to respond, but I finally, said, "It's nice to meet you."

"Are you eating alone?" Ambrose asked.

"No. I'm meeting Lucas Furman and his father here for dinner." I peered over his head but didn't see any familiar faces. Had I gotten the day or time wrong? "Have they arrived yet?"

"Yes. Yes. I apologize for the confusion. They didn't mention they were expecting a guest." Ambrose took my elbow. "Right this way. They're at their usual spot. Please allow me to escort you to their table."

Ambrose's overreaction intrigued me. Was it my place on the council or my family's magic that made the little man so nervous?

Ambrose led me through the diner, until we reached the very back. Huge circular booths took up both corners of the room. Lucas and an older version of him were sitting in the one to the right. The other was unoccupied.

Lucas sprang to his feet and said, "Lexie, it's good to see you again."

His smoky voice floated over me in a wonderful blanket of warmth, and it took me a second to respond, but I finally said, "You too."

He gestured to the man sitting in the booth and said, "This is my father, Quillen Furman. Dad, may I present Alexandria Ravenscraft. The newest resident of our special community."

The man stood and in an accent thick enough to drive cattle said, "Nice to meet you, ma'am."

"Please call me Lexie, Mr. Furman."

"Only if you'll call me Quill." We shook hands, and he gestured to the booth. "Please, have a seat. Do you like beer?" When I nodded, he said, "Ambrose, bring us three bottles of the Newcastle Blood Red Ale."

As I slid onto the padded bench, the diner owner bobbed his head and scurried away, presumably to fetch our drinks. Lucas and his father sat on each side of me and I glanced around for the menus, but the only things on the table were glasses of water.

"Are you settling in all right?" Lucas asked. "It must be hard to pick up and move somewhere like Echo Springs all by yourself."

"It was a bit difficult, but everyone has been very welcoming." It seemed best to keep my answer vague since I wasn't sure how much council members knew about my circumstances.

"That's good." Quill's words didn't match the line that had formed between his eyebrows, but his next ones did. "Just be aware that some folks around these parts aren't exactly what they seem."

"Uh-huh." I wondered if I should come right out and ask about the magic. Or maybe mention the black van that had tried to run me over.

As I contemplated sharing that information, my gaze wondered over Quill's shoulder. Suddenly, I felt tense and jittery.

In the few minutes since my arrival, the diner had filled up. Nearly every seat was taken, and I scanned the room, trying to detect a reason for my agitation. Of the eighty or so patrons, I could only get a read on about half of them. The rest, no matter how hard I concentrated, were blank.

When I returned my attention to the Furmans, Lucas caught my eye and said, "If folks' guards are up, our abilities don't usually work on each other."

"Abilities?" Was he saying what I thought he was saying? It was a struggle, but I managed to keep my expression mildly inquiring.

"You don't have to pretend with us," Lucas assured me. "The council is aware that Elissa planned to fill you in the day after the party."

When I remained silent, Quill patted my arm and said,

"Son, I'm betting Miss Lexie here doesn't quite believe her cousin."

"Oh, right." Lucas tapped his fingers on the tabletop for several seconds, then gazed into my eyes, and said softly, "But you know in your heart that everything Elissa said to you is true."

My chest tightened, and I couldn't catch my breath. When Lucas looked at me like that, it felt as if someone had sucked out all the air in the diner with a vacuum. Was that his ability?

"But..." I opened my mouth, but sadly, nothing intelligent came out.

"Enough of that." Quill patted my arm again and said, "We'll let you get used to things and talk about it again some other time."

I smiled back at him. Lucas' father exuded kindness and warmth, which, in this town, probably meant he was pure evil. But I sure hoped not.

While I was still musing about Quill's true character, Ambrose brought us our drinks. He also handed out menus saying he'd be back to take our order in a few minutes. It was interesting that the diner owner was personally waiting on us while most of the other patrons were being taken care of by a bevy of servers.

Maybe being one of the founding families and a member of the council meant special treatment. I wasn't sure how I felt about that. It might be nice for a while, but I'd bet good money it would get awkward pretty darn quick.

After Lucas made sure I liked the beer his father had recommended, Quill said, "Why don't we figure out what we want to eat, then while we wait, I'll tell you everything I know about your dad?"

Unsure of what I felt like eating, I leafed through the many pages of the extensive menu. As expected by the name of the diner, Wizard of Hogs' meat selection was heavily pig influenced.

Lucas must have noticed my indecision, because he said, "If you like spare ribs, Ambrose's cook is a master of the grill. He makes his own dry rub using brown sugar, mustard, plus six spices he refuses to reveal. And his sauce is 'slap your mama' good."

"Sold." My lips twitched, and I asked, "Are you always this persuasive?"

Lucas shot me a look that, had he been a German Shepherd, might have passed for a grin.

CHAPTER FOURTEEN
Generation Hex

As the evening wore on, I found myself enjoying Lucas' and Quill's company more and more. Quill's reminiscing of growing up with my father was heartwarming. He talked about them playing together as children, as well as hunting and fishing together as teens, which as far as I could tell, took place in the early 1900s.

But my ears perked up when Quill moved on to them as young men and said, "Before your father left on his Saorsa, he was dating Calista Enescu, I thought they'd end up married, but..."

"But he met my mother during his Saorsa," I supplied, then asked, "Is it common to marry people from outside the community and bring them back?"

"No." Quill's bushy eyebrows formed a V over his nose. "And it rarely works out when it happens. The adjustment is just too difficult."

We were silent as we finished the delicious ribs, coleslaw, and fries, then as I was wiping my fingers on my napkin, I asked, "Is the Calista you mentioned my father dating Cole's mother?"

"Yep." Quill took a swig of beer. "She married Tariq Pendergast shortly after your dad returned with Miranda as his wife."

"That had to be awkward." I took a sip of water. "But she got over it, right?"

"Not so much." Lucas twisted his lips. "Let's just say she didn't attend your dad's funeral, and she wasn't sad to see your mother disappear."

"Any chance she's the one who killed my father?" I asked,

129

then put my hand over my mouth. I had to stop blurting out whatever popped into my head. "I mean, I'm sure she didn't, but..."

"Oh, it crossed all of our minds." Quill chuckled. "Except, of course, for my idiot brother-in-law who was sure no one in town was responsible."

"But I thought you all used your powers to keep outsiders from entering the city limits?" Hadn't Elissa mentioned something like that?

"My uncle was sure that someone found a weak spot and slipped past our barriers," Lucas said. "It was just after my aunt left him, and he wasn't in the best of shape psychologically."

"Like he ever was," Quill scoffed. "Denying his abilities is just crazy. That's what drove my sister away, but Neville insists she was unfaithful."

I tucked all the information I had gathered into my mental files and said, "I need to get going, but thank you for a lovely evening."

Both men stood and slid out of the booth. While I settled my purse on my shoulder, some silent communication took place between Quill and his son.

As I started to leave, Lucas said, "Let me walk you to your car."

"No. That's okay." I didn't think being alone with him in a dark alley was a good idea. He seemed like a nice guy, but so had my ex.

As if reading my mind, Quill jumped in and said, "How about if Lucas and I both escort you to your candy store? We can watch from the street to make sure you get to your vehicle all right."

"Fine." I wasn't sure if I was more afraid of the Furmans or the return of the mysterious van. If I hadn't seen Gil go into the river and not come back up, I would wonder if he'd been the driver.

The Furmans were perfect gentlemen, and I was home safe by nine. After making a cup of tea, I sat down with the estate papers. This time I was able to get through two more pages before the headache started. Maybe I really should see the doctor for a checkup.

Giving up, I watched a couple of episodes of *Say Yes to the Dress*, then got ready for bed. Tomorrow, I'd ask one of my customers where in town I could get reading glasses. Either that or just let Uncle Will go over the papers with me like he'd offered.

The phone woke me the next morning at seven, and I groggily answered, "Yes?"

"Did I wake you?" Elissa's cheery voice sparkled from the speaker.

"Um." I sat up and cleared my throat. "I needed to get up, anyway."

"Sorry," Elissa said, then added, "I forget everyone isn't an early bird like me. Anyway, I wanted to warn you that Mom and Dad are back and will be stopping by the candy store to meet you."

"Okay." I wondered why Elissa thought I needed a heads up for that.

"They can be a bit overwhelming, but don't take anything they say to heart."

"Sure." I paused, then asked, "Is your mom mad that I inherited?"

"No. It's not that." Elissa hesitated. "It's... she didn't get along very well with your mother and it may take her a while to warm up to you."

"I understand." Getting out of bed, I grabbed clean underwear from the drawer.

"Anyway. I'll let you go and if you want to talk later, call me tonight."

After Elissa disconnected, I walked into the bathroom and turned on the shower. It sounded as if it would be another interesting day.

Once I was dressed and had eaten breakfast, I had an hour to kill before going to work. Selecting a key at random from Aunt Pandora's ring, I climbed the stairs and when I found the lock it opened. I swung the door inward, then gasped. The room was packed with stuff. It felt like I was on an episode of *Hoarders* as I edged my way through the narrow space between rows of boxes, discarded furniture, and stacks and stacks of old magazines.

If all the locked rooms were like this one, it would take me from now until I was ready to move into assisted living to go through them.

With less than forty-five minutes before I had to head over to the candy store, I wouldn't be able to make much of a dent in the piles of stuff crowding the space. Although, I did manage to drag several broken chairs and about a hundred pounds of National Geographic down the stairs and into the bed of Aunt Pandora's pickup.

Once I was done with that. I cleaned up and drove to the shop. I was still leery of the parking lot, and as I deposited my load into the store's dumpster, I kept a sharp eye out for any threatening vehicles.

It was almost ten o'clock when I finally finished heaving the junk into the trash can and made it inside. After stowing my purse in the desk drawer, I quickly washed my hands and grabbed an apron, retrieved the cash drawer from the safe, and ran to the front of the store to unlock the door and flip the sign from closed to open.

It wasn't as if I expected a long line of customers, but it was a letdown to realize that I had rushed for nothing. As far as I could see, there wasn't a soul in sight anywhere on Main Street.

With no one to wait on, I pulled my cell phone from my pocket. I thought I'd felt a vibration as I'd been hurrying around, and I was right. There was a text from the mayor reminding me that the council was hosting a Spring Ball Friday and as a member I was expected to attend.

Considering that this was the first I'd heard about the ball, reminding was a strange word for him to choose. Informing might have been better, but then again, his message sounded more like a command.

The event started at seven, and council members were instructed to be in the hotel ballroom no later than six-thirty. Evidently, a short meeting would be held before the festivities started.

Without even consulting Uncle Will, I knew that skipping this shindig would get me into big trouble. I swore under my breath when I read that the dress code was black tie. I hadn't packed any gowns and didn't think my one cocktail dress would do. Who knew that I'd need formal attire in Echo Springs?

Shoot! I'd have to stop at Princess Di's, I mean Francine Althorp's clothing store on my way home. I had to pray she had a floor length dress that would fit me. One that wasn't hideous and that I already had shoes that would match would be a real bonus.

The morning went smoothly, and once again, there was a steady stream of customers. As I boxed chocolates and wrapped trinkets, I wondered when my aunt and uncle would show up. After Elissa's warning, it was hard to stop my pulse from racing every time someone entered the shop, but I'd been in retail long enough to keep a pleasant expression on my face even when my heart jumped into my throat.

Having forgotten to bring anything to eat for lunch, my stomach was growling, and I was considering eating a tray of truffles when a little after one the door was thrust open and a striking couple strolled into the store. They looked to be in their early forties, but considering the whole Echo-Springs-citizens-age-at-one-third-the-normal-rate-after-turning-thirty, I figured that despite their younger appearance, they were most likely my aunt and uncle.

They gave each other a look I couldn't decipher, then the woman held out her arms and said, "Alexandria, darling, it's so good to see you. We're your aunt and uncle, but please call us Nora and Bryn."

"Hi. It's nice to meet you."

I wasn't thrilled at the idea of a hug, but I knew I didn't have a choice unless I wanted to look like a real bitch, so I came around the candy display case and allowed myself to be enveloped in a cloud of expensive perfume. After my uncle had his turn, I returned to my original position behind the counter and waited.

"We were so sorry not to be here to greet you when you arrived." Nora adjusted the gorgeous blue pashmina around her shoulders and toyed with her silver necklace. "But I'm sure Elissa took you under her wing and made sure you had what you needed."

"Between her and Uncle Will, I've been taken care of very well."

At the mention of my honorary uncle, Bryn's mouth tightened. It was only for an instant, and his eyes remained expressionless, but I was sure I hadn't imagined his reaction. What about Uncle Will had caused the tension to appear around his lips?

"Well, now that we've returned, I hope you'll call on us for any assistance."

Bryn's lush, thick accent startled me and my aunt must have seen the surprise on my face because she explained, "Bryn is

134

from Mont Pulcianoa, a town in Italy with the same extraordinary properties as Echo Springs. We go there after Christmas and stay through the end of March."

"I imagine the weather is much better there," I said, then searching for something to talk about, I asked, "How did you two meet?"

"There's an exchange program between special towns like ours." Bryn's brown eyes twinkled and reminded me of expensive brandy. "Otherwise the bloodlines would get too genetically narrow."

"People in Echo Springs do marry each other," Nora elaborated. "But enough choose partners from other towns to keep our genes vital."

"Good to know."

We exchanged a few more pleasantries, then Nora said, "We must be off, but we'll see you tomorrow at the ball. You'll sit at our table of course."

"Of course." I agreed, having no idea what my other options might be.

After my aunt and uncle left, the rest of the day was routine. I was happy that no one came in looking for a charm, but the real relief was that no one tried to kill me.

CHAPTER FIFTEEN
Ghouls Just Want to Have Fun

After I closed up for the day, I toyed with the idea of stopping at Uncle Will's before heading to the dress shop. I wanted to know why he hadn't told me about the Spring Ball. But if I showed up at his office he was bound to ask me about the estate papers, so instead, I fired off a snippy text warning him I would need to use the credit card he gave me as I had to buy a gown for the ball he hadn't mentioned to me.

And while I was at it, I sent a similar message to Elissa. One of them should have warned me that there was a formal event that I was expected to attend.

I had checked the Althorp's Fine Apparel Website and fortunately, the store was open until seven on Thursdays. Now if I could just catch a break, Princess Di, I mean Francine wouldn't be working.

Of course, my luck wasn't that good, and she met me as I walked in the door. Her upper crust British accent rubbed me the wrong way, but I pasted a cheery expression on my face and returned her greeting.

After glancing around and seeing that I was her only customer, I looked at Francine and said, "As it turns out, I didn't pack any gowns when I moved here, so I need one for Friday night's ball."

"Oh, my." Her forehead wrinkled under her wispy blond bangs. "I'm afraid I don't have much of a selection in your size." She tilted her head, appraisingly. "You're an eighteen, right?"

"Well," I gritted my teeth, "beggars can't be choosers. And I'm a sixteen unless the designer runs small." Honestly, in a formal gown, she was probably right, but I wouldn't admit that to her.

"I have two in each of those sizes." Francine swept her the center of the store where a small sofa and two matching chairs were arranged. "Have a seat. I'll bring out the evening gowns. I keep them in the back as there isn't usually a lot of call for them."

Once she left, I tried to make myself comfortable on the couch, but the mannequin looking down on the seating arrangement made me nervous. I kept turning around and staring at the faceless woman.

She was wearing black and white geometric patterned capris and a red top. I wasn't sure if it was the lack of features or the fact the top should have been black that bothered me. But something was making my skin crawl.

Finally, I forced myself to stop checking on the mannequin and look around the shop. The walls were lined with racks of clothing organized by color. I was tempted to take a quick look at the tags to see what the prices were like, but before I could get up, I heard footsteps. A second or two later, Francine appeared with a gown in each hand.

I recognized a Ralph Lauren and an Adrianna Papell. The Lauren was a classy black number with a metallic jacquard flared skirt, and the Papell was a blouson in a lilac gray beaded chiffon.

Francine held out the latter gown and said, "This would be a good shape for you, but the color won't be flattering with your fair skin."

"It will wash me out." I nodded my agreement with her assessment. "I'm not crazy about full skirts, but I'll try the Lauren."

"Let me put it in a fitting room for you, and I'll grab the other two."

So far Francine was very gracious, and I wondered if my initial reaction to her was because of my mother's Princess Di obsession. Maybe the snootiness I thought I'd detected in her when we first met was more in my imagination than in any reality.

I was still contemplating my possible bias when Francine returned with a sequined silver gown from a designer I didn't recognize and a gorgeous Aidan Mattox.

She held up the silver one and said, "This is a sixteen, but it runs small."

"It's not really my style anyway and I've never been a fan of silver." I pointed to the other one and said, "But I love the Mattox."

"It's my favorite for you too." Francine beamed. "The cloud blue color will look amazing with your copper hair." She frowned and bit her lip. "Unfortunately, it *is* the most expensive of the four."

"Hmm." I pondered my meager resources, then said. "I still want to try it."

"Yes. You must." Francine clapped her hands and said, "This way."

"Thank you." I smiled and followed her. "It was a relief to see that you were open late tonight. I just found out about the ball this morning and had to wait until after the candy store closed."

"There's always a last-minute customer on Thursday nights." She didn't explain the reason for the Thursday evening rush, instead as she ushered me into a spacious fitting room, she asked, "Now that you've had a chance to learn about the true Echo Springs, how do you like it?"

"It seems like a very nice little town," I answered noncommittally.

"And have you come to accept all the special abilities of its citizens and your place in the community?" Francine stepped out of the dressing room and closed the door behind her, but she spoke through the louvers. "I mean it had to be difficult after growing up with no knowledge of your families' gifts."

"Uh-huh."

I wasn't about to discuss the whole magic situation with her when she might be the one who had talked about killing me at the welcome party.

Turning my attention to the dresses. I quickly shed my khakis and long-sleeved polo shirt, then glanced at my feet and wished I had my high heels on instead of loafers. I knew the Lauren would fit and look okay on me. I'd worn that label before, but I tried it first anyway, saving the one I really liked for last.

Once I slipped the gown over my head, I opened the fitting room door and asked, "Could you zip me?"

Francine obliged, then stepped back, gestured to a raised dais in front of a three-way mirror and invited, "Let's see how you look."

After inspecting myself from all angles, I said, "It fits well and looks nice." And it did, but it wasn't the one that I liked the most.

"Yes, but doesn't do as much for you as I think the other one will." Francine took my elbow and pulled me toward the fitting room. "Go ahead. Try on the cloud blue one and see what you think."

I returned to the fitting room and slipped the Mattox over my head. It had a body-skimming fit through the bust and waist, then flared slightly over my hips. The sweetheart neckline showed enough cleavage to be sexy without being slutty, and the built-in bra meant I wouldn't have to worry about the thin shoulder straps. The A-line skirt was covered in cascading tulle ruffles and would be the perfect length with my three-inch bone heels.

Even before I stepped out of the fitting room and onto the dais, I loved the dress.

Francine zipped me up, then stood back and breathed, "It's perfect." She fingered the gold bangle on her wrist and said, "You look beautiful. You'll have to fight the men off with a stick."

"I really like it." Twirling around, I admired how the ruffles moved.

I should have checked the price when I was in the fitting room, but I'd been afraid to see the number. Now, I took a deep breath and went for it. But as I tried to grasp the tag, Francine intercepted me. I feinted to the left and made a successful grab at it, then turned the little cardboard square so I could see the amount.

I gulped and Francine said, "It is on the pricey side."

You think? Thankfully, I didn't say that out loud, only to myself.

Aloud, I murmured, "I shouldn't spend so much for a dress that I probably won't be able to wear again." I fingered the material. "Even if it is utterly gorgeous and seems to be made for me."

"Maybe we can make a deal." Francine's big blue eyes held a crafty gleam.

"Like what?" I kept staring at my image in the mirror, and I almost felt hypnotized.

"I'll sell you the dress at my cost, and you'll owe me a favor."

"What kind of favor?" I knew that I should say no and take the perfectly nice Lauren dress, but although I like to think of myself as a responsible adult, I tend to lie to myself about stuff like that.

"Nothing awful," Francine giggled. "Just a charm I might

need in the future."

"For what?"

"Why don't you go change into your street clothes and we can discuss this over some bubbly." Francine glanced at her watch. "It's past closing time, so I'll lock up and meet you in the lounge area."

Before I could answer, she hurried away. My mind racing, I carefully took off the gown and hung it on its padded hanger. Then I put on my slacks and top and walked out into the front of the store.

Francine was seated on the sofa and patted the cushion next to her. I sat down, and she handed me a crystal flute of champagne.

"If I promise you I don't want a charm to harm anyone, will that be enough?" Francine took a swallow of the golden liquid.

"I hadn't even thought of that." I wrinkled my nose at the bubbles as I sipped the delicious nectar. "Actually, I'm not even sure I can give you a charm unless it's something you truly need."

Okay. I had vowed not to discuss magic with her, but I caved in with that gorgeous gown dangling metaphorically in front of me.

"It is something I need." Francine's cheeks turned pink. "I suspect my husband is losing interest in me. Or maybe just never loved me as much as I loved him. Now he wants to try for a baby, but I need to know one way or the other before I get pregnant."

"Oh." I thought it over as I drank a little more champagne. It seemed like something that would be all right to use my family's ability to accomplish. And I did want that dress. After a few more seconds of indecision, I wrestled my conscience into submission and said, "That sounds like something I can do. Let me know when you want it, and I'll give it my best shot. But you know that I'm a novice at this charm stuff, right?"

"Believe me." Francine beamed. "Something like what I need will be a piece of cake for you."

As she leaned over to hug me, out of the corner of my eye. I caught a slight movement behind us. Instinct took over, and I snatched her arm and jerked both of us to our feet. A nanosecond later, the mannequin toppled from its stand and crashed into the couch.

Looking at the smashed dummy, I gasped as I saw that her extended right arm had pierced the sofa cushion where I'd just been sitting. If I hadn't gotten out of the way, there was a good chance that I would have been seriously injured.

Francine had been beside me and in the same danger, so she couldn't have been responsible for the mannequin's fall. The shop was locked up, so unless someone was hiding, it had to have been an accident.

Still, I couldn't shake the feeling that this was another attempt on my life.

CHAPTER SIXTEEN
Face the Magic

I had begun to accept that everything Elissa had told me was true. There was just too much evidence and too many Echo Springians who talked about it as if it was a fact to deny it any longer. Unfortunately, now that I was a believer, I was even more uneasy about my new life.

If it was true that I was the Shield of the good magic, it was also true that the other side wanted me dead. And that meant attending the Spring Ball was like walking through a minefield. In snowshoes. Blindfolded.

There were a few other obstacles in going to the dance. One, I either had to close the candy store early or ask Inga to come in since I couldn't work until six and get to the hotel ballroom by six-thirty. Second, I wasn't sure I could drive the truck's stick shift in a long dress. And third, the shoes I had been hoping to wear with my gown must have gotten left behind in Chicago.

Yes, those were more mundane complications than someone out to murder me, but they were still problems. The first two were easily solved. Inga agreed to cover the store from four to closing and Elissa answered my snippy text by offering to drive me to the ball.

That only left the shoe situation. It was six fifteen, my cousin would be by to pick me up at any moment, and I still was standing around in my stocking feet. I held a black sandal in one hand and a bone pump in the other. Neither was dressy enough for the occasion.

Briefly, I tried to use magic to conjure the right footwear, but no matter how hard I concentrated, nothing happened.

Evidently, whatever force controlled my ability didn't think formal shoes qualified as a real need. I'd have to ask Elissa about that.

Wait a minute! Wasn't there a pair of silver high heels among Aunt Pandora's things?

I hurried out to the garage where I had stacked the boxes I'd filled with the contents of her closet. Shoving them around until I found the one I wanted, I tore open the flaps and dug through until I found the pair I remembered. Since we appeared to be so physically similar, I could only hope that my aunt's pumps would fit.

They were a tiny bit big, but I rushed back inside and stuffed the toes with tissue. I was walking around making sure the shoes would stay on my feet when I heard Elissa's car coming up our shared driveway.

Grabbing my evening bag and the lace stole that Francine had given me as a gift to apologize for her mannequin almost shish kabobbing me, I dashed outside. Elissa was behind the wheel of a cute orange MINI Cooper and waved enthusiastically when she saw me.

As I settled in the passenger seat, I was surprised at how roomy the car was inside. My dress and I fit just fine. Almost before I got my door closed, Elissa hit the gas, and I hurriedly fastened my seatbelt.

Rocketing down the street, Elissa beamed at me, then gestured between her dress and mine. "It's almost as if we planned this."

She was right. We were not only wearing the same designer, but our gowns were also the same cloud blue and basic style. But hers had beading and was more fitted instead of flounced. I glanced down at her feet. She had on a gorgeous pair of Badgley Mischka embellished d'Orsay stilettos, and I had to swallow my jealousy before I could speak.

"Did you get yours at Francine's store?" I finally was able to ask.

"Where else?" Elissa shot me a look. "I mean, is it worth risking a couple of days of aging to drive to Kansas City to shop?"

"True."

Suddenly Elissa hit the brakes, threw the car in reverse, and neatly paralleled parked in front of the hotel. I was shocked that we'd gotten such a good spot. Had my cousin used a charm to get it?

Once the MINI Copper was tucked between two large sedans, she shook her finger at me and said, "How long did it take you to be convinced about the magic?"

"Not long enough," I muttered exiting the vehicle. Then as we walked to the door, something dawned on me and I said, "You aren't on the council, right?" She shook her head and I asked, "Then why are you here so early? I thought everyone else had until seven."

"I was in charge of making sure you got here." Elissa's cheeks reddened. "My mom seemed to think you weren't too thrilled about attending, and our family absolutely has to be represented by our council member."

"Oh." I couldn't recall saying anything about not going to the ball to my aunt and uncle, but then again one of our family's powers was the ability to read people's emotions, and I hadn't been trying to block her. Clearly, I needed to work on that.

"I'll hang out at the bar until the meeting is over." Elissa licked her lips. "I can definitely use a drink before the ball starts."

She started to turn off into the lounge area, but I stopped her with a hand on her arm and asked, "Can you teach me how to put up a wall so people can't use their abilities on me so easily."

"Sure." She patted my fingers. "Let's get together tomorrow

145

for a girls' night and I'll show you then." She dug through her purse, pulled out a folded fan, and after murmuring a few words, she gave it to me and said, "If you feel someone nudging you to do something or intruding on your thoughts, hold this up between you and the person."

"Thank you so much." I examined the fan. It was made of antique silk and had tiny blue forget-me-nots painted across its surface. It was obviously valuable, and I said, "I'll take good care of it."

"Don't worry." She waved her hand. "It'll take care of itself." She glanced at the slim white gold watch on her wrist and shooed me away. "You better go. Believe me, you do not want to be late."

With that less-than-reassuring remark ringing in my ears, I followed the signs and hurried toward the ballroom. As I entered, Francine spotted me and waved me over. I nodded, walked behind the table, and slid into the chair next to her.

James Dean, I mean Jeremy Wilson, was on my other side and he gave me a sweet smile, then turned his attention to JFK aka Patrick Fitzgerald aka the mayor, who cleared his throat shot me an annoyed glance, and said, "Now that we're all here, let's begin."

If the mayor had aimed that barb at me, which was highly likely since I was the last one to arrive, he would not get the satisfaction of making me squirm. Anyone who had worked retail for as long as I had developed a thicker skin than being called tardy could penetrate.

Francine handed me a sheet of paper and explained, "Our agenda."

I glanced at the numbered items, but before I could examine them, Patrick motioned toward Cole Pendergast and said, "You have the floor."

Cole, looking unbearably handsome in a Givenchy gold and

146

black jacquard two-button tuxedo stood and faced the group. "Now that our council is once again at full strength, we need to consider how we can help the Echo Springs citizens who have lost their abilities."

I remembered Elissa mentioning that some families' powers had faded, or a generation had kept the information from their descendants so they were unaware of their abilities.

"We have no idea what might happen if we meddled with other's gifts," the woman Uncle Will had told me was Virginia Hensley here, but Patsy Cline to the rest of the world protested.

"Heck, Cole, do we even know how to go about something like that?" Lucas asked.

"There has to be a charm that could help them." Cole looked at me, and everyone else followed suit. "Now that we have a true Shield, it should be within her abilities to provide what they need."

I opened my mouth, but if I had any fantastic words of wisdom to impart my brain refused to reveal them to my vocal cords.

"Perhaps we should give Lexie a chance to settle in and figure out her powers before we ask her to do something that's never been done." Francine bumped shoulders with me. "How does that sound?"

"Good." I squeaked out. "That sounds really, really good."

Patrick rose and nudged Cole out of his way. "I motion that we table this item until Alexandria gives us the green light. All in favor?"

Everyone, even Cole, said aye, then Virginia got to her feet and said, "Next, we have two citizens requesting to go on Saorsa. Faylynn Neville would like to live in Nashville to sing at the clubs and Ezekiel Provo would like to be a priest in the Vatican."

Ezekiel's choice didn't surprise me. My first impression of him had been that he looked more like an angel than a man.

Lucas stood and addressed the council. "I thought we agreed no more celebrity Saorsas." He glanced at Francine, then at the mayor. "Considering the difficulty with the extraction the last couple of times."

Lucas was wearing a Western-style tuxedo and looking just as handsome as Cole did in his Givenchy.

"Faylynn has assured me she won't sign any record contracts and will cut short her time out in the world if she begins to become well known." Virginia's lips twitched. "Are you sure your objection isn't because your uncle will blow his stack if she leaves?"

"That is something to consider." Lucas' tone was neutral. "Do we want to risk our chief of police having a mental breakdown?"

"But is it fair to Faylynn not to allow her to go because of her father?" Jeremy asked. "I vote yes, and if Chief Neville loses it, we remove him from office."

"How about Ezekiel?" Virginia asked. "Anyone have a problem with his application?" No one spoke, and she said, "Okay, I motion that we allow Faylynn and Ezekiel to begin their Saorsas as soon as they're ready."

I abstained and Lucas voted no, but the ayes carried, and we went on to the last item on the agenda.

The mayor resumed the floor and said, "We've had a query from Nimbly, Australia. Because their female population is declining, they would like to send some of their men here to court some of our single women."

Ah. This must be the special town exchange that Aunt Nora had mentioned.

"Why?" I asked, then quickly added, "I mean what's causing the dwindling?"

"Excellent question." Cole gave me an approving smile. "And how many men are we talking about?"

"Three," Patrick said, then looked at me. "And to answer Alexandria, they claim that there is a curse. There have only been a handful of baby girls born in the past twenty years."

"And they don't have enough abilities among them to remove this curse?" I asked.

"Evidently not." Patrick's smile was more of a smirk when he said, "They'd like to talk to you about that while they're here."

CHAPTER SEVENTEEN
The Courtship of the Echo Springs Shield

The council decided in favor of allowing the Australians to visit and have a consultation with me. I again abstained. With that issue settled, they adjourned the meeting, and I fled to the bathroom.

I needed a few minutes alone before the rest of the partygoers arrived for the ball. The idea that not only did the council expect me to help Echo Springs citizens find their lost magic, they also wanted me to undo Nimbly's curse, was overwhelming.

Actually, overwhelming was too mild a way to describe my feelings. In truth, I was seconds away from a full-blown panic attack.

A week ago, my biggest responsibility was finding a client a pair of pants that didn't make her butt look big. Now, two towns were depending on me to perform miracles.

Staring into the mirror over the sink, I was distracted from my looming meltdown by the sight of my hair. How had it gotten to be such a mess?

When I styled it earlier, I'd been going for a sophisticated updo, but evidently, my curls hadn't gotten the message and now hung like a bedraggled mop around my face. Had I been running my fingers through my hair without even realizing it?

Lucky for me, the hotel's ritzy powder room provided hairspray among several other items wealthy women expected to have at their fingertips when attending fancy events. With the help of several pins and half a can of Aqua Net, I got my curls under control and back on top of my head. I had to quit playing with my hair when I got nervous.

After applying a new coat of Bobbi Brown pale pink lipstick, I took a deep breath, straightened my shoulders, and marched myself back to the ballroom. I had barely crossed the threshold when Cole appeared next to me and took my elbow, guiding me over to an older couple standing next to a table of hors d'oeuvre.

Cole gestured to the pair and said, "Alexandria, I'd like you to meet my mother and my father, Calista and Tariq Pendergast."

We shook hands and exchanged pleasantries, then Calista said, "You look so familiar." She tilted her head. "Have we met before?"

"I was in Will's office earlier in the week and you passed me as you were leaving." I hadn't thought she saw me as she stomped out the door, but maybe she'd caught a glimpse despite her snit.

"No. No." She tapped her fingers on her chin all the while staring at me, then smiled. "That's it! You look exactly like your aunt. The Ravenscraft genes are very dominant. I don't see any of your mother's in you at all." Calista took a sip of something clear, and I didn't think for a minute it was Seven-Up. "Which is a good thing. Miranda's weakness nearly brought down your family."

My tongue tripped over my response and the noise I made sounded as if I'd taken a gulp of lemon juice with a shot of lime on the side.

"Don't deny it." Calista took another sip of her drink, then refocused her gaze on me.

"From what I understand, Mom had good reason for everything she did. Especially moving away." It wasn't as if I didn't know my mother had faults, but I wouldn't let anyone else say so.

"That was the least of it," Calista snapped. "If she hadn't refused to acquire the abilities Pandora offered her, she could have helped protect your father, and he'd never have died." Her voice broke. "It was selfish of her."

"Now, now, dear." Tariq put his arm around his wife and murmured in her ear.

Tariq was an older version of his son. No less appealing and no less powerful. But the lines around his eyes and mouth told me he was a lot craftier.

Calista continued to protest whatever her husband was saying, until Cole said, "Mother, why don't we talk about this more tomorrow at brunch when you and Alexandria will have more privacy."

"Capital suggestion." Tariq beamed at his son, then said, "In fact, why don't we escort the ladies to the dance floor? The two most beautiful women in the room shouldn't be standing here like wallflowers."

Cole immediately asked, "May I have this dance, Alexandria?"

I nodded and cautiously allowed him to take my hand. There was that same odd tingle as when he'd touched my palm at my welcome party, but at least this time, I didn't feel faint and pass out at his feet.

We made our way to the front of the room, and I was thankful that the band was playing something slow. I'd never had lessons of any kind and could only hope I could follow his lead.

I slid into his arms and we started moving. My sense of rhythm wasn't the best, but Cole's must have been amazing. He twirled me around the dance floor and never once allowed me to step on his feet.

After a few minutes, he said softly, "I'm sorry about my mother."

"Believe me, I understand." I leaned back so I could look into his eyes. "It seems as if my presence upsets her. Maybe we should cancel brunch."

"Absolutely not." Cole's tone was firm. "You and she need to talk this all out so we can all be on the same page. It's not good for any of the seven families to be at odds with one another."

"Okay, but although my mom wasn't by any means perfect and made some mistakes, I won't allow your mother to blame her for everything."

"All I ask is that you listen to what Mother has to say and perhaps share some of your story with her." Cole brushed a curl out of my face and smiled. "I very much want you two to get along."

"I'll do my best for the sake of the town and its citizens." I had been holding my evening bag in the hand resting on Cole's shoulder, now I switched it to the other one. That was one of the things I hated about dancing. I never knew what to do with my purse.

"That's not the only reason I want you and Mother to become friends." Cole pressed his lips to my temple, and the tingle running through me turned into an electrical charge down my spine.

Before I could react, a large hand tapped Cole's shoulder, and a deep voice said, "My turn."

I lifted my head and met Lucas' brown eyes. Cole hesitated, then with a final squeeze reluctantly relinquished his hold on me. Lucas immediately slid his arm around my waist and took my hand, causing a similar, yet distinctly different tingle to shoot through me.

Once we started dancing, Lucas said, "I hope you don't mind me cutting in, but otherwise, Cole would have monopolized you all night."

"I doubt that very much." Glancing around the ballroom, I chuckled, "After all, it's not as if I'm the only single woman here."

"Just the most beautiful." Lucas' voice lowered to a rumbling purr.

"Well, thank you," I shook my head, "but we both know that's not true."

"Eye of the beholder," Lucas murmured in my ear as the music stopped.

He stared at me as if daring me to say anything else, then when I was silent he escorted me to a table occupied by his father.

After saying hello to Quill, I sat down on the chair Lucas held for me. As he slid me closer to the table, I twitched my dress into place.

I was still fussing with the flounces on the skirt when a middle-aged woman with a thick brunette braid and darkly tanned skin strolled up to us. She dropped a kiss on Quill's head and nodded at me.

She was carrying two tall, slender glasses, and handed me one as she said, "Hi, I'm Lucas' mother, Ramona." She took the seat between Lucas and Quill and smiled. "I hope you like prosecco."

"Love it!" I was surprised. Prosecco wasn't exactly a common wine. I tasted it, and the light, delicate, fruity, and floral flavors were immediately identifiable as my favorite kind. "Is this Mionetto?"

"Of course. Your raven told me it's your preferred brand."

"My raven?" I asked sure I'd misheard her.

"You'll meet him later." Ramona's dark honey eyes twinkled, and I had just taken another sip of wine when she added, "He came to me first because he knew I'd want to make sure to get the best for my future daughter-in-law."

154

The prosecco blasted down my trachea, and I choked, then gasped, unable to catch my breath. Lucas leaped to his feet and gently thumped me on the back.

When he sat back down, he glared at his mother who smoothed the lace sleeves on her dark orange gown. Although she seemed unconcerned at his censure, I could see the muscles on her biceps tighten.

Lucas continued to stare until Ramona lifted her eyes, then through gritted teeth he said, "I thought we agreed not to make Lexie uncomfortable."

"Why would me saying I wanted to please your betrothed, make our darling Alexandria uncomfortable?" Ramona's expression may have been innocent, but I could hear the craftiness in her voice.

"Because we only met a few days ago, and I haven't proposed yet?"

Taking a gulp of much-needed air, I was probably just about to say something marvelously clever, but I couldn't remember what had been in my head because Lucas' words had completely shut down my brain.

I glanced at Quill, who was obviously the king of deadpan. Too bad maniacal is more my speed, and I'm sure my own expression was crazed.

With three pairs of eyes focused on me, my mind raced for an appropriate response and I finally said, "Well, it's a shame then that I already have a fiancé."

The momentary panic on Lucas's handsome face was worth the points in heaven I'd just lost for lying.

"Just kidding," I smirked then quickly got to my feet and said, "Thank you for the wine, but I should mingle."

As I walked away, I heard Quill's voice say, "You better fix that right quick."

Assuming he meant Lucas needed to repair things with me,

I increased my speed and scanned the room for a safe harbor. My best bet was my uncle and aunt, especially since Elissa was with them. I briefly wondered why I hadn't seen Uncle Will at the ball, but his absence slipped my mind as I zoomed over to my family's table.

The three of them welcomed me with broad smiles, and as she gestured to the empty fourth chair, my aunt said, "You're just in time, dear. The staff will serve dinner any second now."

"Terrific." Although it hadn't occurred to me that there would be a meal, it made sense. I hadn't eaten dinner, so I was hungry, but after my encounter with the Furmans, my stomach was tied in knots.

When the waitress brought our salads, I used the distraction to whisper to Elissa, "You will never believe what just happened."

"What?" She kept an eye on her parents who were debating the merits of balsamic vinaigrette over classic Italian dressing.

"Ramona Furman said I was her future daughter-in-law." I kept my voice low.

"Well, that's surprising." Elissa shook her head. "I would have expected the first volley to come from Calista."

"The first volley?" Once again, I had no idea what was happening.

"Oh. Yeah." Elissa slapped her forehead. "I didn't explain that you were promised as a bride to either the eldest male Furman or Pendergast."

"Promised?" Evidently, all I could do at this point was echo my cousin's words.

"When your dad married outside of the community, to secure our family's continued place on the council, he had to promise his firstborn's hand in marriage to one of the other founding families. The Pendergasts and the Furmans are the only ones with male heirs."

156

"What happens if I fall in love with someone else and marry him?" I asked.

"Banishment." Elissa's features darkened. "For all who have the blood of the Ravenscrafts."

CHAPTER EIGHTEEN
Cut to the Witch

I stuck it out at the ball through dinner, which would have been delicious if I hadn't lost my appetite, then persuaded Elissa that I needed to leave. As we were leaving, I spotted Uncle Will at the bar with a group of older men I didn't recognize.

He smiled and nodded at us, but returned to his conversation without beckoning us over. Which was fine with me, as I was more than ready to go home.

The five-minute trip was silent, but as I got out of the car Elissa said, "I know this is all a lot to take in, but we'll talk about everything tomorrow night. Come on over to my place around seven. We'll watch chick flicks, eat stuff we shouldn't, and I'll answer as many of your questions as I can. Until then, don't worry."

"Sure, why should I be concerned that someone wants me dead? Or the council expects me to perform magic on command. Or that my father evidently agreed to a forced marriage for me before I was even born?"

"It'll be fine." Elissa's smile was gentle as she waved and drove away.

Although I was exhausted, I was sure I couldn't sleep, so after I changed out of my finery and washed my face, I grabbed the estate papers and got into bed. I made it through four whole pages before my eyes started to droop. Up to this point, at least as far as I could tell, it seemed standard. And with only a couple of more pages to go, I was confident I could get it finished, signed, and ready to drop off at Uncle Will's office by Monday.

As I slipped into an uneasy rest, a series of nightmares

began. The final one, the one that woke me screaming, was of me standing at the altar between two men. The lace on my veil was so thick I couldn't see any details, but when the ceremony was over, the groom dressed in black lifted my veil over my head and I saw that he had a wolf's head with gleaming red eyes. Then, as he leaned in to kiss me, he'd unhinged his jaws revealing razor-sharp teeth he buried in my throat.

Sitting up, I clutched the blanket to my chest and took gulping breaths trying to calm my racing pulse. My heart thudded in my ears as the scene played over and over in my mind.

When I could finally breathe normally, I looked at the bedside clock. It was only six a.m., but there was no way I wanted to go back to dreamland, so I swung my legs off the mattress and got up.

I briefly toyed with the idea of going shopping downtown, but I wasn't ready to be in another crowd of people. Maybe after I'd talked to Elissa and had a better understanding of everything in my new life, I'd look around the various shops.

That left me with seven hours to kill until I had to face one of my prospective bridegrooms... and his mother. With any luck, that would be enough time to finish the room I had begun cleaning out on the second floor.

I threw on an old pair of sweats I'd found among Aunt Pandora's things, pulled my hair into a high ponytail, and after my usual breakfast, I headed upstairs. As I opened the door, my heart sank. I'd forgotten what little progress I'd made the other day.

Sighing, I started the first of many trips to the garage, hauling out the rubbish.

When I stopped at eleven-forty-five. I could see the lovely hardwood floor. The only items remaining were a beautiful antique sleigh bed and the matching dresser. I wasn't sure what

I'd do with them, but I certainly wasn't throwing them into the trash.

The hot shower felt amazing on my sore muscles, and I hated to get out. Once I forced myself to turn off the water, dried off, and wrapped the towel around me, I walked over to my closet. Now that I knew about the marriage promise, I needed to look put-together, but not as if I was flirting.

Deciding to go with classy and chic, I pulled out a knee-length cream lace skirt and a muted peach chiffon blouse. Again, I wished for my nude pumps. How in the heck had I overlooked packing them?

I settled for off-white ankle boots with a two-inch heel, then attempted to replicate the style Harmony had coaxed my hair into at her shop. That went pretty well, but it took me a bit longer to do my makeup since I had to cover the dark circles under my eyes.

Still, I was ready by quarter to one. Driving the truck in a skirt was a challenge, but I managed and once again parked behind the candy shop.

When I entered the restaurant at precisely five minutes before I was due, the hostess who evidently had been warned to watch out for me, popped out from behind the podium and said, "Ms. Ravenscraft, this way, please."

I followed her down a hallway and when she paused at a massive oak door, I waited a few steps behind her as she knocked and announced, "Ms. Ravenscraft is here."

The door swung open and Cole, wearing a beautifully cut black suit with a blue shirt that matched his eyes, nodded at the hostess, "That will be all, Greta." As she disappeared down the corridor, he turned his attention to me, stepped back and said, "Please come in."

The room was small, with a lovely stone fireplace, a leather sofa and wingback chairs, and a large table with four place settings. It smelled of old money and ancient power. Calista was already seated at the table and gazing into what appeared to be a full martini glass. It seemed as if she was looking for an answer to a difficult question. I held back a chuckle. I mean, I knew alcohol was famous for solving problems, but usually you had to drink it first.

She raised her head and gave me a cool smile, "Alexandria, my dear, how nice of you to join us."

Was she implying that I was late? I frowned, then forced my lips to curve upwards. "Thank you for inviting me. I love a good brunch."

Her icy blue eyes swept my body, and she said, "So it would seem."

Evidently, I was not the prospective daughter-in-law she had envisioned.

"Mother." The warning in Cole's voice was clear, and Calista gave a tiny shrug. He stared at her, then as he assisted me into my chair, he said, "You look lovely. Is that skirt a Ralph Lauren?"

"Yes, it is." I put my purse next to my leg and commented, "You certainly know your designers."

"I spent some time in New York during my Saorsa." He seated himself between his mother and me, then added, "And while I was there, Mother had me picking up clothes for her at every showroom."

"You didn't object to meeting all those models or escorting them to all those parties." Calista raised a perfectly groomed eyebrow. "And who can blame you, they all were so slim and lovely."

"Mother, either behave, or Alexandria and I will have brunch alone."

"Fine." Calista shot me a look that said she was only stopping because her son insisted, then asked, "Did you enjoy the ball?"

"It was nice to meet more Echo Springians," I answered cautiously.

"I noticed the Furmans tried to monopolize you." Calista sipped her drink.

"They were just being friendly." I picked up the crisp white linen napkin in front of me and placed it in my lap.

I was trying to pretend that I was as dumb as a box of rocks, not acknowledging the marriage sweepstakes between the two families. Sadly, it wasn't as hard as it should have been. For a straight A student, I'd been acting pretty stupidly the last couple of weeks.

Suddenly, I wondered if when Gil attacked me and slammed my head into the floor, instead of getting away like I remembered, he'd actually inflicted brain damage on me. Maybe all this business about magic was just a dream I was experiencing in my comatose state.

"Alexandria?" Cole's voice brought me back to the present, and I jerked my mind into submission.

"Sorry." I noticed that without my noticing, a server had entered the room and was now offering me a drink from the tray she carried.

"Would you care for some champagne black raspberry punch?" Cole asked. "It's one of our head bartender's brunch specialties."

"Sure." I helped myself to a glass and tasted it. "Wonderful."

When a second server placed a plate in front of me, Cole said, "The chef grows his own greens and strawberries for our salads."

"Impressive." I waited until Cole, and his mother had their plates, and the servers left, then forked a bite into my mouth. "Yummy."

"You know, it was foretold that your father would be the strongest Shield in Echo Springs' history." Calista ignored her food and drank deeply from her martini glass. "He and I were supposed to have married and together eliminate the dark magic from our town forever." She tilted her head back a couple of inches, as if imagining what might have been, then said, "But Nathanial was selfish."

Various emotions plugged up my throat, and I couldn't force out any words. Sorrow at never knowing my father. Mortification that my family had failed in its destiny. And anger that Calista was blaming me.

Once again Cole stepped in and said, "Mother, Alexandria is not responsible for Nathaniel's actions." Then, before Calista could respond, Cole continued, "Nor is she responsible for Miranda's."

"That woman ruined everything." Calista scowled at me. "Your mother, refused to transform. She promised your father she would become a true Ravenscraft, then she reneged. And when Nathaniel threatened to divorce her over it, she got pregnant with you."

"Oh." Calista's accusation stunned me. I wasn't sure they were true, but knowing my mother, I couldn't completely dismiss the allegations.

Cole opened his mouth, but a knock on the door interrupted whatever he was going to say, and instead, he called out for the server to enter. Our next course was a delicious salmon and asparagus frittata with a slice of corn quiche on the side. Too bad my appetite had disappeared with Calista's denunciation of my parents.

When the three of us had our food, and the server closed the door behind her, Cole said, "I apologize for my mother." He shook his head and tsked. "What she failed to tell you is that Dione later admitted she might have read the signs wrong, and it wasn't Nathaniel and my mother who were intended to eradicate the dark magic."

"That is, in fact, true," Calista, said before taking a bite of her frittata.

She had agreed too readily, and I immediately tensed waiting for her next volley.

"In fact," Calista said slowly. "Dione now believes it was Nathaniel's daughter and my son, who are the soulmates destined to save us all."

Her gotcha expression reminded me of a Chihuahua my mother had owned. It was the same look he'd give me after peeing on shoes—but only my favorite pair.

A genuine smile finally relaxed Calista's sharp features, and she announced, "Which is why it is vital you choose my son and not Ramona Furman's whelp."

CHAPTER NINETEEN
A Witch's Tale

Instead of waiting for my reply to her latest mindboggling statement, Calista rose majestically from her seat and swept out of the room without a backward glance. Cole didn't seem perturbed by his mother's behavior, but my mouth hung open long enough that I was lucky we were indoors or I might have swallowed a fly.

I finally gathered my wits and asked, "Was she serious?"

"As a stake in the heart." Cole took my hand. "It's no secret that if you choose the correct mate, you and he will gain great power."

"And if I choose incorrectly?" I half closed my eyes afraid of the answer.

"Then it will be up to the next generation to correct your mistake."

"Well," I blew out a thankful breath, "then that's not too bad."

"Actually, it might be." Cole drained his champagne punch, then reached under the table and pressed a button I hadn't noticed before. "The problem is that with every failed generation, the dark side grows stronger."

I shuddered and Cole was silent. We were both relieved when there was a knock on the door and two servers entered. One poured coffee while the other placed our desserts on the table. After we assured both of them that we didn't need anything else, they left us alone to eat our whipped ricotta with honey and mixed berries.

As I added cream and sweetener to my cup, I decided to channel Scarlett O'Hara and think about it all later when I could discuss what I'd been told with my cousin. My aunt had warned me not to trust anyone else and with every passing second, it seemed like better and better advice.

Taking a deep breath, I force a smile and said, "This dessert looks wonderful. How about we enjoy it while we talk about something a little less dire than the entire future of Echo Springs?"

"Certainly." Cole picked up his spoon. "Neville mentioned that you were an aspiring actress before coming here. We have a community theater group you might be interested in joining."

"That sounds fun." I had lied to the chief about my career goals, but I had been in several college productions. "When are the next tryouts?"

"I believe they're in May."

"Terrific." I smiled. "That'll give me time to settle in first."

Cole and I kept our conversation light while we finished eating, and when he walked me out to my truck, he made an elegant gesture as he opened the driver's door for me. It reminded me of the footman in Cinderella. I was delighted until I remembered that in reality, the footman in that story had been a rat.

It was only a little past three when I got home, but I was beat. So instead of doing something productive, I scrubbed my face clean of makeup, changed into an oversized T-shirt, and crawled into bed.

Usually, I couldn't sleep during the day, but I must have been exhausted because I didn't wake up until a few minutes to six. After I indulged in my second shower of the day, dried my hair, and applied some blush and mascara I dressed in my favorite Ideology leggings and tunic.

Unwilling to go to Elissa's empty-handed, I dug through the freezer until I found a carton of Haagen-Dazs butter pecan ice cream. Loading it and a bottle of Hershey's chocolate syrup into one of the cloth shopping bags I'd found in the pantry, I walked over to my cousin's.

Elissa met me at the door, gave me a hug, then as she ushered me into her kitchen said, "I hope you're hungry, I'm making pizza."

"Making?" I asked sniffing appreciatively. "Like from scratch?"

"Uh-huh." Elissa went behind the island and picked up a grater and a hunk of cheese. "When I found out I was celiac, it was easier to learn to cook gluten-free than trust restaurants."

"That explains why you passed on the rolls last night." I thought back. "And why the bread for our sandwiches at the library was homemade."

"Yep." Elissa finished topping the homemade crust and slid it into the oven. "I usually, bring my own dinner rolls when I eat out, but I didn't have time to make any."

"So even though we age at about a third of the rate as normal people, diseases like celiac can still affect us?" I asked.

"The short answer is yes." Elissa wiped her hands on a towel. "If you never leave Echo Springs, the conditions never surface, but they do if we go on Saorsa."

"So, as long as nothing has come up with me so far, if I don't go back into the outside world, I'm safe?" I was suddenly glad I'd had to have a thorough physical when Crystal changed insurance plans.

"Theoretically." Elissa shrugged. "We've never had someone raised away from town before."

"Hmm." Another thing my mother was responsible for doing to me.

"What's in the bag?" Elissa nodded toward the cloth tote I still held.

"Ice cream and syrup." I handed it to her. "I hope it's okay for you to eat."

"Let's take a look at the ingredients." She studied both labels. "Haagen-Dazs is usually fine unless it contains cookies or brownies and Hershey's chocolate products are generally good too."

"Phew."

After pronouncing my food contributions safe, Elissa said, "The pizza will be ready in ten minutes. Let's grab plates, silverware, and napkins and get set up in the living room. You can pick out a movie from my collection."

"Sounds great." I browsed through my cousin's DVDs and chose *The Devil Wears Prada*. The Meryl Streep character reminded me of my old boss. Although Crystal may not have been a warm and fuzzy mentor, compared to the world, I'd suddenly found myself in, she was a pussycat.

We settled in to watch the movie and were silent until the timer beeped. While Elissa took the pizza from the oven and sliced it, she asked me to get the bottle of Sauvignon Blanc she had chilling in the fridge, as well as the wine glasses from the counter.

Once we were seated on the sofa again, this time with slices of veggie pizza on our plates, instead of starting up the movie, Elissa said, "You must have a thousand questions. Do you want to just talk while we eat?"

"That would be awesome." As my mind whirled trying to figure out where to start, I took a bite of the pizza, savoring the peppers, olives, onions, and mushrooms on the crisp crust. Swallowing, I said, "I can accept most of what I've been told the past week, but the part I'm really having trouble with is the whole good versus evil magic." I took a sip of wine. "Oh. And the whole thing about me having to marry either Lucas or Cole. Is that actually true?"

"Yes, and no." Elissa snickered when I rolled my eyes. "Yes. Your father did promise your hand in marriage to one of the council families' heirs."

"How about Jeremy Wilson or the mayor?" I wasn't interested in either man, but I wondered why they weren't in the running.

"Patrick was already married at the time your father made his promise, and Jeremy would have only been a possibility if your father had had a son. Although how two men could combine their DNA to produce an heir is beyond my current knowledge, I'm sure there's a way." Elissa wrinkled her brow, then shrugged. "Anyway, that leaves Lucas and Cole as the only two candidates."

"Oh." I pondered this new information while I drank more wine, then asked, "This afternoon at brunch, Calista Pendergast told me that some woman named Dione predicted that Cole was my soulmate and that he and I are destined to permanently eradicate the dark magic."

"Dione Chaz is our oracle." Elissa's lips quirked in a parody of a smile. "What she said was that according to the flight of the doves, the Shield and the Silver Sword would combine to defeat the corrupt magic."

"Who is this Silver Sword?" I frowned at this new information.

"As soon as Dione announced her prediction, Calista dug out a picture of one of her ancestors holding a silver sword."

Elissa chugged the rest of her Sauvignon Blanc before adding, "But then Ramona produced documents showing that the Furmans have been the guardians of a plant called the silver flame, which is also known as the silver sword."

"How accurate are Dione's prophecies?" I asked, then followed Elissa's example and polished off my wine.

She poured us both another glass and said, "I'd guess about seventy-eighty percent. She sure was right about my poor choices."

Well, shoot! I realized that all our conversations had been about me. I'd never asked my cousin anything about herself. I truly was a selfish bitch.

It was time to mend my ways, so pushing away the rest of my questions and concerns, I said, "Do you want to talk about it?"

"There's no need. Getting you up to speed in your role as the Shield is more important than my disastrous attempt at dating."

"So you want me to bare my soul to you, but you don't want to share anything about you with me?"

Elissa's brows shot into her hairline, but she didn't duck the accusation. "You're right. I'm so used to keeping everything private because the Ravenscrafts aren't allowed to show any weaknesses."

"Well, now you have a cousin, so spill it." I selected another slice of pizza and waited.

"There was this guy who came here from a Canadian town like Echo Springs," Elissa said, taking a sip of wine between each word. "He was an English teacher, and we hit it off over our passion for books."

"What happened?" I prompted, a little concerned at how quickly my cousin was going through the bottle of Sauvignon Blanc.

"My mother didn't think he was worthy of a Ravenscraft and Dione told me he wasn't the one meant for me, but I didn't believe either of them." Elissa shook her head. "I should have seen the light when he rhapsodized about his Hoover and bought me a DustBuster for my birthday."

"But you didn't?"

"No. By then I wasn't about to admit to everyone that they'd been right."

"What convinced you to end it and deal with the fallout?"

My cousin's self-awareness impressed me, considering her alcohol level.

"I caught him boinking the Hallowell sisters in the women's room of the library. All three of them!" Elissa snorted. "So now I don't date."

"You've sworn off men altogether?"

"It's not that so much, as I just have more respect for my vibrator."

"Okay then." I giggled and reached for the bottle of wine. It was empty, which was probably for the best.

"Enough about my pitiful love life." Elissa got to her feet and carried our dirty plates into the kitchen. I followed with the rest of our trash, then helped her dish out the ice cream. After we'd thoroughly covered the multiple scoops in our bowls with chocolate syrup, we returned to the sofa, and Elissa said, "What other questions do you have?"

I once again put on my Big Girl Panties, the ones that were starting to bunch up and irritate me, and said, "I've decided to find out who killed my father. Any ideas of where I should start?"

"You should start by not stirring up that pot."

I could tell by Elissa's voice she wasn't expecting me to heed her advice.

"Fine." I gave her a look that meant I was still going to investigate, but I wouldn't expect her help. "In that case, how about the attempts on my life?"

"Already?" Elissa squeaked.

I explained about the van trying to run me over and the mannequin falling, but when she seemed relieved, I demanded, "Why aren't you more upset about it?"

"Because it couldn't have been the ruler of the dark magic. He or she has to be touching you when they kill you." Elissa licked chocolate sauce from her spoon. "Whoever was driving the van or pushed over the mannequin was just your run-of-the-mill bad guy."

CHAPTER TWENTY
Charmed to the Teeth

My mouth felt like I'd been chewing on used kitty litter and the pins and needles in my legs caused me to sink to the floor when I tried to stand. It took me a second to remember where I was and what had happened, but then I squinted over at my snoring cousin and dredged up the memory of our girls' night in.

Elissa hadn't been able to explain Ramona Furman's comment about *my* raven, but after finishing our ice cream, Elissa had taught me how to block other people's magic from working on me. Still, since I was such a beginner, she told me to keep the fan she'd loaned me.

She also showed me one other spell that didn't require a specific charm. If I was in mortal danger, I could send a mental distress signal to all my blood relatives and my fated soulmate.

I hoped I wouldn't have to use it, but on the other hand, it might be the only way I'd ever figure out who I was really supposed to marry.

Once we finished with my magic lessons for the night, Elissa opened another bottle of wine and we watched the rest of the movie. I'm a little fuzzy, but I think it was when I asked Elissa about my father's murder again that she brought out a third bottle.

Either she was drunk enough to throw caution to the winds, or she knew that I wouldn't let the matter drop, but Elissa finally told me to talk to the owner of the bookstore. She said he'd been the one to find my father's body.

I had tucked the piece of information into a corner of my brain just before Elissa and I both passed out on the sofa. And now that I was awake, I repeated it to myself as I stumbled to the bathroom, splashed my face with water, drinking some from my cupped hand, and then peered out the window into the bright sunshine.

What time was it?

Shoot! I had to open the candy store by ten.

Rushing back to where Elissa still sawed logs on the couch, I found my purse under the coffee table and dug out my cell phone.

Phew! It was only a few minutes after nine.

Still, I had to hustle if I wanted to wash and down some caffeine before work. I quickly wrote Elissa a note thanking her for everything, put it on her chest, and let myself out the door.

There was no time to primp today, so after the world's fastest shower I scraped my wet hair back with a headband. Juggling a travel mug, my makeup case, and my purse, I ran for the truck.

As I drove to the shop, I applied concealer under my bloodshot eyes and gave my lashes a few swipes of mascara. If I wasn't too busy with customers, I might be able to put on some bronzer and eyeshadow later.

I arrived at the store at nine-forty-nine, dismayed to see that people were already lined up at the entrance. And from the moment I opened the front door until I flipped the sign to read CLOSED at six o'clock, there was a steady stream of shoppers. I had no idea why so many Echo Springians needed candy so badly, but several made a point to mention seeing me at the ball.

Evidently, my presence there, and being recognized publically as a member of the council, was great for business.

After I locked up the Candy Box I strolled over to Spellbound. It was a relief that the hours printed on the door said the store was open from noon to eight p.m., and as I crossed the threshold, I saw several people browsing the shelves.

Knowing how badly bookstores in general, and indie stores

in particular, had faired the past several years, I was thrilled that Echo Springs had one at all, let alone, by all appearances, one that was going strong.

It made me think about something that hadn't occurred to me before. Did Amazon sell out here? I mean, if the residents' magic managed to stop outsiders from entering the town, how did anything get delivered?

I knew there was mail because I'd seen Aunt Pandora's bills and letters, all of which had a United States postal stamp on them. But maybe the other services like FedEx and UPS weren't allowed.

Then again, businesses needed supplies. Some delivery firms had to be able to get into town. I pursed my lips, trying to remember if I'd seen invoices for the candy store merchandise anywhere. I thought I had, but as soon as I got home, I would check.

Why was it that as soon as I got one set of questions answered about my new life, another bunch cropped up?

Frowning, I pushed aside that mystery for the time being and walked toward the counter. The man behind the register was short, with a pointy face, and skinny arms and legs. He looked a little like the hamster from the Kia Soul commercial, and as I approached, his mustache twitched as if I had distracted him from a run on his exercise wheel.

Holding out my hand, I smiled and said, "Hi, I'm Lexie Ravenscraft."

"I know who you are." He glanced at the people absorbed in their hunt for the perfect read, then said, "I'm Hamilton Digger, the proprietor of Spellbound Books. Welcome to Echo Springs."

"Thank you." When he failed to shake my hand, I dropped it to my side and said, "I'm so thrilled to find a bookstore in my new hometown."

"What genre do you like?" He asked, his small dark eyes

looked into mine.

"My tastes are fairly eclectic." I leaned a hip against the counter. "I'm not too interested in nonfiction, but almost anything else."

"Hmm." Hamilton dashed out from behind the register, scurried down an aisle, and a moment later returned with a paperback copy of a mystery with a cover featuring a snowman wearing a hat and tie and a snow woman with a peach ribbon around her throat and waist. The store owner thrust it at me and said, "You should read this."

"Sure." I dug in my purse for my wallet and pulled out my credit card. "But I really wanted to talk to you about my father. I understand you found his body, and I was hoping you could tell me about it."

"Read the book." Hamilton said, "The printed word is always the best source of information."

That reminded me that my eyes kept getting blurry when I tried to examine the last couple of pages of the estate papers. I glanced down at the point of purchase products on the counter and spotted a rack of reading glasses. Removing a pair from their cardboard display, I put them on top of the novel.

Before I could hand my charge card to him, Hamilton plucked it out of my fingers, ran it through his machine, and returned it to me along with a bag containing my merchandise. Then the strange little man turned his back on me, making it clear our conversation was over.

Wondering if I would ever understand the citizens of Echo Springs, I headed to my truck and drove home. Through the twilight, I could see lights glowing from the windows of the houses I passed, and loneliness struck me square in the chest. I was in a strange town among people I couldn't trust. How had this happened?

It was past seven by the time I walked into my kitchen and I was starving. In my rush to the candy store this morning, I'd missed breakfast and had candy for lunch. No wonder I was feeling so maudlin. My blood sugar was probably crashing harder than a race car that missed a turn going two hundred miles an hour at the Indy 500.

After scarfing down a huge turkey and cheddar sandwich, and half a bag of potato chips, my mood improved. My plan for the rest of the evening was to veg in front of the television, but even after I changed into sweats and a T-shirt, I couldn't get comfortable.

The cushiony couch that had previously been so restful seemed lumpy and my gaze kept wandering up to the ceiling. Suddenly, there was a strange pressure between my shoulder blades and I felt compelled to get up, climb the stairs, and enter the room that was next on my list to be cleared out, that is once I rented a dumpster.

Entering, I inched past the maze of furniture and boxes until I reached the opposite wall. There, clear of the clutter that filled the rest of the space was an old trunk. It was made of wood with odd characters carved across the top.

I squatted and studied the ornate lock. It was brass with beautifully raised details. As I ran my finger over the strange swirls and random stylized shapes, I realized that there was no keyhole.

Maybe it wasn't a lock after all. I inserted my fingers under the latch and tried to flip the lid up, but it held firm. Sitting back on my heels, I examined every inch of the trunk and the lock. My gut told me I needed to get into it, but intuition told me that damaging the antique chest was a very bad idea.

Could this be something I was supposed to fix with a spell? I concentrated. What had keys that didn't need a keyhole to function?

My mind was a blank. It was getting late, and I was drained.

I should go to bed and deal with this tomorrow when my brain was working better.

Heck! I could ask Elissa if she had an idea of how I was supposed to unlock the trunk.

Standing, I turned to leave, but I couldn't make my legs move. I glanced over my shoulder at the chest and could swear it was smirking at me.

I sank back down on the floor, glared at the trunk, and muttered, "Fine! You want me to open you; I need some help here."

Long minutes went by, and my eyelids began to droop. My chin hit my chest, and I jerked awake. It was time for bed, and as I got shakily to my feet, I caught a movement out of the corner of my eye.

Squinting, I saw the carved characters rearranging themselves. I held my breath as they moved, then blew it out in a long puff of air when I realized the shapes had come together to form letters that had spelled the word PIANO.

What in the heck was that supposed to mean? There was no piano in the house. At least, not anywhere I'd seen. And if I did find one, how would that open the trunk. Was I supposed to play it?

It wasn't as if I'd had lessons. Mom never had the money for that kind of extra. So any sound I produced wouldn't be musical.

Dejected, I walked out of the room only partly aware that my legs were working again. At least I had that going for me.

I was halfway down the stairs when a memory flickered at the edge of my mind. I *had* seen a piano in the house. Just not a full-sized one. There was a miniature of the instrument in the night table beside Aunt Pandora's bed."

CHAPTER TWENTY-ONE
Spell Bent for Trouble

Feeling a little silly talking to an inanimate object, I held the miniature piano in my palm, offered it to the trunk, and said, "Here you go."

Nothing happened.

I placed the tiny instrument on the lid and feeling even more ridiculous asked, "This is what you wanted, right?"

Nothing, again.

Squatting down, I peered at the lock and the carvings, looking for an indentation or slot where I could insert the piano, but I didn't see anything.

Next, I examined the piano. It was carved in exquisite detail with no sign it was anything other than a solid piece of wood, shaped and painted to resemble a baby grand.

Since my dignity was already in shreds, I tried rubbing the piano, then wishing on it, and finally blowing on it. But neither it nor the trunk seemed at all affected by my actions. In fact, I had the distinct impression they both were sneering at me.

Sinking to my knees, I let my mind go blank. I was nearly asleep when I heard myself recite, "It takes eighty-eight keys to unveil the magical music of our family. Black and white. Old and young. Large and small. Reveal to me what is hidden."

With a quiet whir, the lock twisted sideways, and the lid popped up. I eagerly leaned over the lip to look inside. The trunk was filled with dozens and dozens of clear plastic cubes, each containing a single object.

I could see twisted bits of hair, a goblet that looked as if it was made from a horn, vials of salt, a horseshoe, and a four-leaf clover in the top layer of boxes. Next to them was an old notebook.

Carefully extracting it, I gently eased open the brown leather cover. On the first page, in faded blue ink and written in a spidery cursive was a short poem that read:

MAGICAL OBJECTS ALL.
CHOOSE CORRECTLY TO PREVAIL.
ONCE, ONLY WILL THEY ANSWER YOUR CALL.
CHOOSE UNWISELY, AND YOU FAIL.

Evidently, I had discovered the Ravenscraft charms. Now I just had to figure out how to use them. Surely one of them could help me find my father's killer.

As I fingered the different cubes, unable to see how they opened, I heard the thump of footsteps starting up the stairs. A flame of fear sizzled through my chest.

Who was marching toward me as if he or she had every right to be here? And why was my cellphone still in my purse, which was uselessly sitting on the kitchen counter?

Involuntarily, I gripped one of the Lucite cubes and the lid popped open. I took out the contents and examined the lemon-sized brownish-black rock that fit my hand perfectly.

It had a metallic luster that seemed to glow brighter just before I slid the stone into the pocket of my sweatpants. Quickly flipping the pages of the notebook, I searched until I found the word protection.

I hastily memorized the two-line verse, then put the notebook in the trunk and closed the lid. The lock reengaged a nanosecond before the door to the room opened.

Standing there, still alive, was Gil. His skin was ashen, his smile demented, and his first words were like an icepick in my spine.

"Miss me?"

"I saw you go in the river," I stuttered. "I thought you were dead."

"The current washed me up on shore a few miles downstream." Gil shrugged. "A nice old man found me and nursed me back to health."

"How did you get here?" I was beginning to suspect the magical wards that were supposed to keep random people from wandering into Echo Springs didn't work as well as everyone thought they did.

"Once I was strong enough, nothing could keep me from you." Gil strode over the threshold and marched toward me

Shuffling backward as far as I could go, which sadly was only a few inches, I wrinkled my nose at his stench. He smelled as if he hadn't showered since the last time I saw him and his filthy shirt looked suspiciously like the one he'd been wearing when he'd driven off the bridge.

"You need to leave." I put my hand on his chest and shoved him away.

He captured my fingers and brought them to his mouth. As his mouth pressed against my skin, it was all I could do not to deposit my semi-digested turkey and cheese sandwich on his muddy loafers.

"Don't be like that," Gil tsked. "I came to apologize for my bad behavior and tell you I forgive you and want to start over."

"You. Forgive. Me?" I sputtered. "You tried to kill me. Twice!"

"Only because you were being so unreasonable." Gil frowned, then his brow smoothed. "If you promise not to do that again, we'll be fine."

I was speechless. Did he really think we could go back to being a couple?

"Look," Gil said. His lips quirked up the slightest degree, and I noticed they had an odd bluish-purple tint. "Let's pretend we just met and tomorrow we can go out on our first date."

"You want us to date?" I freed my hand from Gil's grip and

edge my way around him until he no longer blocked my exit.

Intellectually, I knew that people never saw themselves the way others did. The distance between their image of themselves and reality was too wide a chasm for them to leap. The price of honesty about their own shortcomings was too costly to their egos. But still, Gil was obviously delusional.

"Sure." Gil followed me as I backed into the hallway. "I like it around here, and I'm thinking about hanging out my shingle."

"Here?" I had to turn to walk down the stairs, and it seemed an eternity until I reached the bottom. Gil was right behind me with a goofy smile on his face. "We already have a lawyer in Echo Springs, and I don't think there's enough business for two attorneys."

"He's getting old." Gil shrugged, keeping close to my heels as I retreated to the kitchen. "In fact, I might just buy his practice once I get access to my money again."

Not really listening to Gil's ramblings about his future plans, I murmured uh-huh and uh-ah as I made a beeline for my purse.

Although Gil appeared calm, and sort of rational, I kept a wary eye on him while I thrust my hand into the depths of my purse. My fingers skimmed the cool plastic surface of my cell.

Now came the tricky part. I had to remember where both the mute and the speaker buttons were located. This was still a relatively new phone to me, and I hadn't studied it very thoroughly yet. Holding my breath, I made my choices, then by feel, I dialed 911 and trusted the dispatcher would figure out what was happening in time to send help.

While I was distracted, Gil had closed in on me again. He cupped my cheek, and if anything, he smelled worse than he had a few minutes ago. It took all of my willpower not to slap away his hand.

"Gil," I deliberately mentioned his name hoping that if Chief Neville was around, he'd remember our conversation about my ex. "I'm still not clear how you got into my house. I locked the doors, and I didn't hear any glass breaking or wood splintering."

"I have my ways." Gil's smug smile made the bile rise in my throat.

"Well, considering the lateness of the hour and the fact you've tried to kill me twice, if you're truly sorry, I want you to take your hands off me and leave." I'd watched enough crime shows to know the importance of making it clear that I was saying no. "I'm not comfortable with you being here or with you touching me."

"That's too bad." Gil's tone was contrite, but it didn't match his expression. "Because I'm not letting you out of my sight again."

"I thought you said we'd start over and go on a first date." I edged backward until my butt hit the countertop. I glanced at the back door, wondering if I could make it to the truck before Gil caught me. "Sleepovers do not occur on the first date."

"You must have five or six bedrooms in this place." Gil's gaze scanned the ceiling as if he could see through the plaster. "I'll bunk in one of them until you come to your senses." He shook his head, regretfully. "But since you still don't seem to understand that we're destined to be together, I can't trust you so I *will* have to cuff you to your bed."

"No way." My skin crawled. "I didn't let you do that kind of thing when we were a couple, and I'm certainly not allowing it now."

"Here's the thing." Gil's hand shot out and grabbed my wrist.

Shoot! Why weren't the police here? Echo Springs was tiny; their response time should literally be less than five minutes. I listened intently, but couldn't hear any trace of a siren. I should have gone for a weapon instead of the phone. Where had I put the knife I'd used to cut my sandwich in half?

Gil must have realized what I was thinking because his grip on my wrist tightened and he repeated, "Here's the thing. You really don't have a lot of say in the matter. I won't rush you, but I can't allow you to make a poor choice and try to leave me again."

I felt behind me. I was pressed up against a drawer I hoped contained utensils. Maybe I could stab Gil in the eye with a meat fork and make a run for it.

In an attempt to distract him while I eased open the drawer, I asked, "Were you the one in the black van who tried to run me over?"

Confusion crawled across Gil's pallid face and he shook his head. "When did that happen?"

"A few days ago."

"Are you sure someone didn't just mistake the gas for the brake?"

"Of course I am!" I continued my quest for a sharp cooking gadget. "You sound like the police chief. He didn't believe me either."

"Someone is probably paying him off." Gil narrowed his bloodshot eyes then beamed and said triumphantly, "See! You need me to protect you."

"Would that you could," I murmured, thinking the first person I needed protection from was Gil.

I finally got the drawer open and slid my hand inside. But instead of the feel of cold metal, my fingers touched soft cotton.

Great! I suppose I could try to stuff a dishcloth down his throat, but since I doubted he'd stand there and let me do that, escaping out the door was now my only option.

Although I took off running, sadly, I didn't make it two

steps before Gil grabbed me by the waist wrapped me in a restraining bear hug, and shouted, "I'd hoped you'd realized by now we're soulmates."

"No, we are not!" My voice sounded a little like I was channeling Satan or at least his daughter, but I was sick of trying to pacify him. I could speak my mind and be murdered or suffer silently and still end up dead.

"We are." Gil tightened his arms until I couldn't take a deep breath. "Either we'll be together in this world or in the next one."

As he squeezed my body against his, I felt the rock I'd slipped into my pocket just before Gil appeared. It was supposed to be a protection charm, and I definitely needed it in this situation.

Although I was lightheaded from lack of oxygen. I shoved my hand into my pocket and touched the rock. Now if I could only remember the verse to activate it.

How did it go? Something about being set in stone.

Intent on recalling the poem, I nearly blew my chance to get away. But once the significance of the sound of breaking glass forced itself into my consciousness and I felt Gil's grip on me slacken, I raised my knee and thrust it into his crotch.

When he yelped and jerked backward, I sprinted out of the kitchen and toward the front door. I nearly collided with Lucas and Cole before I skidded to a halt.

Instead of saving me, they were standing in the foyer glaring at each other, so I had to shout to get their attention. "Help! My ex is trying to kill me!"

Gil was a nanosecond behind me, but my would-be heroes took the time to shoot one last scowl at each other before they charged him. Gil somehow eluded both of them and snatched the back of my shirt before I could make it out of the front door.

He reeled me in like a fish on the end of a line and held a knife to my throat. Evidently, since I could smell the turkey on it, he'd found the one I used to cut my sandwich in half. You know, the one I should have grabbed instead of going for my cellphone.

Instinctively, I plucked the rock from my pocket and recited, "Set in stone. Never alone. From the ground. Let safety be found."

As I uttered the last word, Gil's hand dropped away, and he fell to the floor. Although, he appeared dead, he'd fooled me once before, so I swiftly took the knife from his hand and yanked a cord from a nearby lamp. Both Cole and Lucas just stared at me as I secured my ex's hands behind his back.

What were they looking at? Hadn't they ever seen a lawyer tied up in knots before?"

CHAPTER TWENTY-TWO
Trial by Magic

"What do you mean I shouldn't call the police?" I'd been headed towards the kitchen to get my cellphone, but I stopped and stared at Cole.

"Neville doesn't take things like this very well." He arched a golden eyebrow. "It's better for the council to deal with it."

"Things like what?" I asked over my shoulder as I ignored Cole's advice and continued on my mission to retrieve my phone. "A stalker breaking into someone's house?"

"Lexie." Lucas shoulder checked Cole out of his way and followed me down the hall. "Just listen to us before you do anything."

"Fine." I turned to face him and glanced nervously toward the foyer where my ex was tied up on the floor and with any luck really dead this time. "Enlighten me. But I have to warn you, it's too late. I dialed 911 a while ago." Frowning, I added. "In fact, I can't believe they aren't here yet."

"The call didn't go through." Cole joined Lucas and formed a wall of attractive men in my hallway. "We heard it, but no one else did."

"Would you care to clarify how that happened?" I crossed my arms. "And why?"

"Well, I, that is, we were worried about you," Cole explained.

"So, you..." I impatiently waved my hand for him to continue.

Lucas took over. "The council sanctioned the use of a spell on your phone."

"Seriously!" I screeched. "Talk about an invasion of

privacy."

"Just until you're more skilled with your magic," Cole soothed.

Lucas stepped forward and put a hand on my arm, but I shook it off. "It only works if you dial 911, then it rings on my cell."

"And mine," Cole interjected.

"And his," Lucas agreed.

"Then you two heard my conversation with Gil?" I asked, still trying to grasp the situation. "And instead of getting the cops, you came to rescue me?" I shook my head. "But why?"

"I," Lucas started, then amended, "I mean we, want to keep you safe until you have command of all your abilities and can take care of yourself."

"After all," Cole flashed me a devilish grin. "You are destined to marry one of us."

Ignoring that last bit, I returned to the original discussion and asked, "If you don't want to involve the police, what do we do with the dead man in my foyer?"

"That's the thing." Cole moved, so he was standing beside me. "Your ex-boyfriend isn't exactly a man. At least not anymore."

"Okay." I held on to my patience, but it was fraying. "He's now a body."

"True." Lucas stepped to my other side. "But more correctly, he was a zombie."

"Then why didn't he try to eat my brains?" I'm not sure why that was the first question to pop out of my mouth, but I let it stand.

"Not a movie zombie," Cole corrected gently. "A corpse reanimated through magic to do its master's or mistress' bidding."

"Somebody found my dead ex, resurrected him, and sicced

him on me?"

"Yeah." Lucas shrugged. "I'd say that pretty much sums it up."

"Who?" I looked at the two men, but neither seemed eager to answer me.

"Probably whoever killed your father," Cole offered hesitantly.

"Right." Lucas ran his fingers through his dark hair. "It's doubtful that it's the…, uh," he paused and glanced at me as if to gauge my reaction, then continued, "you know, other side trying to wipe out The Shield. You're nowhere near producing an heir and gaining your full power, so killing you wouldn't do them any good."

Hmm. This was the first time anyone outside of my family had mentioned, as Lucas put it, the other side. Did that mean he was one of the good guys? Or was he just trying to fool me into thinking that?

"As was mentioned," Cole slid Lucas a disapproving glance. "The fact that you've been investigating your father's death hasn't gone unnoticed."

"That means if we figure out who murdered my dad, we'll figure out who sent Gil." I pursed my lips, then turned, walked into the kitchen, and started a pot of coffee.

Cole smiled and said, "Cream and two sugars for me." He glanced around. "Do you have any cookies?"

"Black for me." Lucas inhaled deeply, then headed toward the pantry. A few seconds later, he reemerged with a package of Pecan Sandies and said, "My favorite."

"I take it you two are planning to help me figure out who's after me?" When Lucas and Cole nodded, I grabbed three mugs from the cupboard near the Mr. Coffee and said, "Then have a seat."

Lucas grinned, then said, "Yep. We might as well get

comfy. It's going to be a long night."

They both headed toward the kitchen table, but before they sat, I said, "Wait. How about the zombie in my foyer?" Boy, that was a sentence I never expected to have to say outside of a nightmare.

"Already taken care of." Cole dusted off his hands. "One of my men will remove it and deal with the remains."

"How..." I trailed off. I hadn't seen him send a message, but I was beginning to figure out how things around here worked, and I guessed he'd communicated telepathically, so I changed what I was originally going to ask and said, "How will your guy dispose of the body?" I didn't want a second encounter with an undead Gil.

"He'll bury your ex in a little cemetery the council maintains just outside the city limit." Cole walked over to where I was standing and patted my hand. "He'll make certain that the means to reanimate him is removed."

I opened my mouth to ask what he meant, then closed it when I realized that I didn't want to know. Sickening images from various zombie movies danced through my head, but I pushed them aside and envisioned a peaceful interment with perhaps a minister blessing Gil's earthly remains.

After we all had a mug of coffee and a stack of cookies, Lucas said. "Tell us about the attempts on your life since you've arrived in Echo Springs."

"First, there was the black van that tried to run me over behind the candy store." I held up one finger. "Chief Neville assures me that no one within the city limits drives the vehicle I described to him."

"I'm going to assume you couldn't see the driver." Cole took a sip of coffee.

"Correct. The windows were too dark, and I was too surprised."

"We could try searching the nearby towns to see if a van like that was reported stolen or rented by someone," Lucas offered.

"We could, but my guess is whoever 'borrowed' it made sure the owner never even knew it was missing." Cole's blue eyes sparkled. "At least that's what I'd do if I could cast spells."

"Wait a minute." I hastily chewed and swallowed the bite of cookie I had just taken, then demanded, "You mean not everyone in Echo Springs can do that?"

"Actually," Lucas frowned, "now that you mention it, only a very few of our people's magic include spells and charms, especially ones that can create a zombie. It would have to be one of the witch families." The crease between his eyebrows deepened. "Which means, we can eliminate about ninety percent of the population."

"My cousin said we didn't use the word witch," I glared at Lucas who shrugged.

"The council avoids the W word because, like the term zombie, it's been corrupted by movies and books," Cole explained.

"What kind of abilities do you two have?" I blurted out, then when neither man spoke, I wondered if that was considered a rude question like enquiring about someone's income or weight.

"I wouldn't be able to force anyone to do something they didn't want to." Lucas shot a pointed look at Cole. "But he could."

"True. I could impose my will on someone." Cole didn't seem upset that Lucas had outed him. "But it would only last a short while."

"Hmm." Evidently, neither guy was going to expound on their abilities, which seemed unfair since they knew mine. "Okay. But how can I be sure that neither of you are the head of the dark magic?"

"You can't," Cole drawled, then smirked when Lucas gave him a live-ammo glare. "We can tell you we aren't, but we could easily be lying."

"Didn't we decide that it was highly unlikely that the attempts on Lexie's life were connected to that issue?" Lucas ate a cookie in one bite, then stared at Cole and me waiting for our reply.

"We did." I sighed. "Anyway. The second attempt was in Francine's dress shop. A mannequin fell from a pedestal, and nearly shish kabobbed me." Before they could ask, I added, "Francine was sitting right next to me, the store was locked, and there was no one else there."

"That could be a family with the ability to move objects from a distance." Cole stroked his chin. "But it could also be a witch family."

"Who have you talked to about your father's murder?" Lucas asked.

"You two and your parents, Elissa and her parents, and Hamilton Digger." I searched my mind for anyone else. "And Inga."

"Inga's abilities are limited to transporting herself from one spot to another, but she can't be in two places at the same time." Lucas said thoughtfully. "And you said she opened the door as the van passed by."

"Hamilton's gift is pairing the right book with the right person." Cole crinkled his forehead. "It's hard to explain, but if someone is stuck in their lives, Hamilton can help them move forward."

"Shoot!" I glanced at the package sitting next to my purse. "He made me buy a book and said something like it would answer my questions."

Lucas got up and fetched the bag, handing it to me as he

reseated himself.

"Thanks." I accepted the sack.

"See if you can figure out what it's supposed to mean." Cole encouraged.

Reaching into the bag, I took out the paperback and the glasses. Once I settled the readers on my nose, I opened the novel and tried to skim through it, but the words were all blurry. "Darn! I'd hoped these glasses would help, but I still can't make out a thing."

"You're awfully young for readers." Cole raised his eyebrows. "Are you sure you need them?"

"I've been having trouble reading the last few pages of my aunt's estate papers so I figured they might help."

"Try the book without the glasses," Lucas advised plucking them from my face.

Irritated at his presumptuousness—we weren't on intimate enough terms for him to be invading my personal space like that—my first inclination was to snatch the readers from his fingers. But considering the situation, I did as he suggested and was surprised to discover that the print was crisp and clear. I gave both men a thumbs up, then started to skim.

I must have been taking too long, because Cole said, "I see that the book is a mystery. Maybe just read the denouement."

His suggestion made sense, so I flipped to the last couple of chapters and hastily scanned for the solution to the crime.

Once I found it, I raised my head and said, "The lawyer did it." My shoulders dropped. "Hamilton must have been warning me about Gil, my ex was an attorney."

"Damn!" Cole tapped the tabletop with his nails.

As the three of us sat in silence, disappointed that the book hadn't been of any help, my mind whirled.

Suddenly, propelled by the thought that had popped into my head, I leaped to my feet and raced into the family room. There, I snatched up the estate papers from the sofa, then returned to my seat at the kitchen table.

Flipping to the next-to-last page of the document, I tried to read it. The print jumped around, and when I attempted to focus, my head throbbed.

Cole and Lucas were watching me with puzzled expressions, and I hastily explained, "I just remembered something Gil said. He told me that the person who rescued him from the river was a nice old man. I'm going to guess that the rescuer was actually the person who turned him into a zombie."

"Seems reasonable," Lucas said, and Cole nodded his agreement.

"Gil also mentioned that the town lawyer was getting old and he might buy the guy's law practice." I watched as the lights began to dawn behind Cole and Lucas' eyes, then added, "And I informed one other person about my intention to find my dad's killer."

"William Mayer!" Cole exclaimed. "An attorney, like the murderer in the book."

I thrust the estate papers at Lucas and demanded, "Can you see the words clearly?" When he nodded, I said, "Start at the second to last page and tell me what it says."

We all gasped when Lucas finished reading and said, "This says that if Lexie dies before coming into her full power, she agrees to pass on the Ravenscraft estate to William Mayer."

Cole stroked his chin and said, "Which would mean neither Elissa nor her parents could make a claim."

"But how much can it be worth?" I asked, unable to believe the man who had told me to call him Uncle Will and been so kind to me was behind the attempts on my life.

"Upwards of five million dollars." Cole said, then when Lucas looked at him in surprise, he added, "What? It's common knowledge that the Ravenscraft abilities include a gift for investing in the stock market."

"But..." I stuttered. "Would Uncle Will really need Aunt Pandora's money?"

"Mayer might be from a witch family, which was how he spelled the estate papers so you couldn't read them," Lucas explained. "But that family's magic is a lot weaker and less reliable than the Ravenscrafts' powers."

"He must have sent Gil here to force you to sign the documents," Cole said. "Doubtlessly he was getting tired of waiting for you to give in and sign them without reading the last couple of pages."

"Uncle Will said he would read the papers to me if I was having trouble," I whispered. "He could have told me anything."

"Good thing you didn't sign," Lucas drawled, then added, "I think you better stop calling him uncle."

I nodded sadly. Despite having magical powers, my ability to judge men hadn't improved one bit."

CHAPTER TWENTY-THREE
Payback's A Witch

"The attempts on my life had nothing to do with my abilities," I exhaled loudly. "It was pure greed."

"Even when magic is involved, people's motivation stays the same," Cole murmured.

"Yep," Lucas nodded. "Sex, money, or power."

"So how are we going to bring Unc... I mean Will, to justice?" I asked.

"That will be tough." Cole crossed his legs, then adjusted the crease in his expensive dress pants. "We'll need to get him to confess."

"Yeah." Lucas frowned. "The council will want hard evidence."

"The council?" I glanced between the two men. "Not Chief Neville?"

"If the police arrest him, he'd have to go to the county court system." Cole tilted his head at me clearly, waiting for me to catch on.

It took me a second or two, but the lightbulb in my head finally popped on, and I said, "Oh yeah. Because that would mean a long trial outside of Echo Springs where a vengeful defendant might reveal our special abilities, right?"

"Yep." Lucas tapped his nose. "Got it in one."

"The Echo Springs police department keeps the town peaceful, but all serious offenses are decided by the council." Cole stared into space, then refocused and added, "Defendants are allowed to be represented by an attorney and can ask for a jury of their peers with the head of the council acting as the judge."

"Can I use a spell to get Will to tell the truth?"

"Maybe, if you were at your full power, you could breach his defenses," Cole said slowly, then shook his head. "But even then the council would disallow the confession on the grounds it was coerced."

"Looks like we'll have to do it the old fashioned way," I murmured.

"And that is?" Cole took a sip of his tepid coffee and made a face.

"We'll trick him into admitting everything, and I'll record it." I narrowed my eyes and concentrated on coming up with a plan.

It took us a couple of hours to figure out how to accomplish our goal. Finally, we decided that I'd make an appointment for the next day telling Will that I was coming by to drop off the signed estate papers. Lucas and Cole would arrive a few minutes after me and stay in the waiting room just in case I needed them. Which was highly likely, since my scheming honorary uncle would probably try to kill me as soon as he had the documents.

My job was to get Will to tell me he murdered my dad before he added me to his list of victims. But just in case he succeeded in offing me, I didn't want him to get the money. So instead of me signing on the dotted line, Cole did it for me with Lucas as a witness that the signature wasn't legally mine.

We forged Elissa and Inga's names as witnesses, and fortunately, Cole was a notary public. He ran home to get his seal, then returned and affixed it to the document. Then we all took a moment to admire our forgery.

It was after two a.m. by the time Lucas and Cole left, but the adrenaline must still have been buzzing through my veins because I wasn't tired. Still, I climbed into bed and shut my eyes.

As soon as I woke up, I was supposed to call Will and make

an appointment for early afternoon, then text my bodyguards with the time. We'd meet in the candy store parking lot and they'd watch me until I walked through the law office door, then after giving me a few minutes to make it into Will's inner sanctum, they'd arrive separately so as not to tip off Ezekiel that anything was amiss.

We didn't think he was a part of Will's plot, but better safe than sorry.

As I tossed and turned, I thought about my upcoming confrontation with death. It was a shame I had used the protection charm on Gil and that each item was only good for one spell.

If I lived, I definitely had to learn how to make my own charms. There were a lot in the trunk, but they'd eventually be gone, and I needed to be able to replace them with fresh ones.

I must have eventually dozed off because when I opened my eyes, the sun was streaming through the window, the clock read ten-thirty, and I had a pounding headache. It almost felt as if I had another hangover, but I hadn't touched a drop of alcohol since my girls' night with Elissa so I chalked it up to lack of sleep.

As promised, after a quick shower, I called Will's law office. Ezekiel told me Will had an opening at one. I dutifully texted Cole and Lucas with that information, and we agreed to meet in the candy store parking lot at twelve-fifty.

Afraid this was my last day on earth, I treated myself to pancakes with lots of butter and syrup, then deciding I wanted to look my best, I took my time getting dressed. With my hair styled and my makeup applied, I pulled one of my favorite outfits from the closet.

As I wiggled into my white denim straight-legged jeans, I hoped this wasn't the last time I'd get to wear them. Next, I slipped into a navy and white striped dress shirt and topped it off with a powdered blue, thigh length, sweater coat. I usually wore heels with this ensemble, but flats would be way better if I had to make a run for it, so I chose my Chuck Taylor low top sneakers instead.

Having donned my warrior apparel, I headed to my rendezvous with destiny. Which evidently would take place in a small-town lawyer's office. Not exactly the way I had pictured myself facing it, but hey, what can you do?

Lucas and Cole were already waiting for me when I parked the truck, and with assurances they would keep me safe, I marched out of the lot, down the sidewalk, and inside Will's building.

Ezekiel greeted me with a wave and pointed toward Will's office. I smiled my thanks and gingerly approached the partly open door.

Lightly rapping on the wood, I called out, "Are you ready for me?"

Will's jovial voice answered, "Of course, my dear. Come on in."

As before, my snake-in-the-grass pseudo uncle was behind his desk. He was talking to someone on the phone but held up his index finger to indicate he'd be with me in a minute, then gestured for me to take a seat.

I nodded my acceptance, then when he returned his attention to the conversation, I quickly opened my tote bag and swiped the record icon I had added to my cellphone's home screen that morning.

Hearing Will say goodbye, I hastily withdrew my hand and rested my fingers on top of the tote bag in my lap. With my best retail smile pasted on my face, I glanced up at the man who had destroyed my childhood and waited for him to say something incriminating.

When it became clear that I wasn't going to speak, Will

cleared his throat and said, "So, I understand you're ready to complete the paperwork for your aunt's estate. Do you have it with you?"

"Of course." Watching him closely, I withdrew the document from my tote bag and said, "Sorry, it's taken me so long, but there must be something wrong with my eyes, or the print is just so tiny. It seemed that by the last page or so, everything was blurry."

His mouth quirked upward for less than an instant, but he immediately straightened his lips and said in a kind voice, "Would you like me to read that page to you before you sign?"

"No. Thank you, but that's all right." Making sure my expression was ingenuous, I said, "I trust you, so I already signed them."

"Excellent." Will couldn't mask his eagerness as he reached for the document and flipped to the pages that required signatures, but a flicker of unease marched across his face as he examined them. "I see you already had this witnessed and notarized. I could have done that for you."

"No problem." I shrugged innocently. "Cole mentioned he was a notary and since Inga and Elissa were in the store at the time and he had his seal, I thought what the heck. I might as well get it all done nice and legal in case something happened to me."

"Although, I'm sure you have nothing to worry about," naked greed blazed in his eyes, and the ratfink licked his lips, "it's better to be safe." He smiled, his little apple cheeks pink. "And as it happens Ezekiel is probably already gone, he had to run an errand for me, which means we'd have had to round up a couple of witnesses. So your having taken care of that was probably for the best."

"Awesome." I figured he'd sent his assistant away so there wouldn't be any witnesses around when he killed me.

"It seems as if everything is in order." Will's voice reeked with satisfaction.

"Well, I should probably get going." I started to stand to see what he'd do.

"How about we have a celebratory glass of champagne before you hurry off?" Will suggested, getting up and going over to a credenza where a green bottle was nestled in an ice bucket. "It's not every day you officially become a wealthy heiress."

"Aunt Pandora was worth that much?" I pretended surprise. "Wow!"

"Well, not to be immodest, but I've been handling the Ravenscraft finances for years, and under my guidance, your family has done very well." He popped the cork. "Very well, indeed."

I noticed Will blocked my view as he poured the champaign into the glasses so I figured there was a good chance he'd put something lethal in mine. He was such a weasel, I'd guessed that poison would be his weapon of choice rather than a gun or knife where he might have to get his hands dirty. I knew that I would have to make him think I was drinking it without actually ingesting any and had come up with a plan to fool him.

Will handed me the flute and returned to his chair. After he was seated, he leaned across the desk and motioned for me to clink glasses.

Once I complied he said, "To Echo Springs newest multimillionaire."

Doubtlessly he meant himself.

As I raised the flute to my lips, I gasped and gestured behind the sneaky snake staring at me. When he turned to look where I was pointing, I quickly poured a quarter of the champagne on the floor.

Turning back to me, Will asked, "What's wrong? I don't see anything."

"There was a huge spider dangling from a web," I lied

smoothly.

"Oh." Will frowned. "I'll have to get the exterminators in here."

"Can't you use a spell?" It was time to surprise him into talking.

"Uh." Will's eyebrows leaped into his hairline, which considering its location was quite a jump. "Who told you about my abilities?"

"A couple of little birdies," I answered coolly as I pretended to take a sip of bubbly.

"So you've been asking around about me?" Will looked bemused, which I had to admit was his best fake expression so far.

"Hmm," I answered noncommittally, hoping to egg him on. "You did seem a little too good to be true. I wanted to see what was in it for you."

"And did you?"

"I think so," I answered coyly. "Sending Gil wasn't your best move."

"Gil?" Will pretended confusion but evidently recognizing my disbelief he shrugged. "It was worth a shot. How did you deal with him?"

"Maybe I've learned more than you realized." I poured a little more champagne out when Will abruptly scooped up the estate documents and tucked them in a drawer as if afraid that I'd grab them. "Now how about you explain why you killed my father."

"I suppose there's no harm." Will's eyes no longer twinkled; instead, his gaze was as icy as a glacier. "Did I ever tell you that my undergrad degree was in chemistry? No?" He smirked. "Well, you've just drunk my own special brand of poison. You'll notice you can no longer move. You'll be dead within minutes."

"Before I die, please tell me about my dad." Sinking back in my chair, I wondered if I had missed my calling. I was turning out to be a much better actress than I thought. "Why did you kill him?"

Will's voice was low and soulless. "Nathanial figured out I was skimming money from the Ravenscraft accounts. I talked him into giving me a day to tell Pandora myself then surprised him and stabbed him in the heart."

"You took away my dad's life, and now I'll take away your freedom. Leaping up from my chair, I snarled a grin, then raised my voice. "Cole, Lucas, I have his confession."

As the guys burst through the office door, Will gasped, "You should be minutes from death by now."

"Sadly for you, I'm fine." I glanced pointedly at the pool of liquid near my feet and added, "But your hardwood will never be the same."

EPILOGUE
The Lie Is Cast

After a hastily called and lengthy council meeting, where I played the recording I'd made of my ex honorary uncle confessing to killing my father and attempting to kill me, Will was safely locked away in the council's jail. The setup consisted of a spell-proof cell and a guard named Serb who looked like a mixture between a dog and a snake.

No one mentioned turning Will over to the police or even notifying them about what had happened. It wasn't any wonder that Chief Neville wasn't too fond of the magical element in his town, even if he was one of them.

Now Cole, Lucas, and I were back at my house, preparing a late dinner for the four of us. No. I didn't miscount. Elissa had been waiting on the porch when I pulled in the driveway. Word had already gotten around that Will had tried to poison me, so she wanted to check if I was okay.

Once we filled her in on Will's entire plot, she ended up joining us as we cooked supper.

"I still, don't understand how Will thought he'd get away with poisoning me in his office." I looked between the two men who had taken over my kitchen and assigned my cousin and me to making a tossed salad while they whipped together the rest of our meal. "Was he planning on nonchalantly carrying my dead body out the front door and stowing me in his trunk?"

The men shrugged, but Elissa said, "Rumor has it there was a black van parked behind his building. There were industrial sized trash bags and a shovel inside, and rental papers in the name of Gilbert Osborn." She raised a brow at me. "Isn't that your dead ex?"

"Yep." I explained the whole Zombie Gil episode, then said, "Okay. Will was planning on burying my body somewhere, but without proof of my death, how could he collect his inheritance?"

Cole looked up from sautéing onions and mushrooms and said, "He'd have to wait seven years from when you disappeared, then he could have you declared dead."

And all during that time, he'd still be controlling the estate and could continue skimming money off the top." Lucas added without pausing in his seasoning of the four rib eyes lined up on the counter.

"He would have never gotten his hands on the full estate. My parents would have fought tooth and nail to prove that the document he had Lexie sign wasn't valid." Elissa shook her head, tsking. "And it's not as if Will's abilities would be any match to my mother's since she'd have the Shield's power if Lexie were dead."

"Aunt Nora would know I had died even if there was no body?"

"Yes. She'd experience a sort of electrical jolt." Elissa looked at me and asked, "Do you recall something like that? You should have felt it when Aunt Pandora passed away."

Shrugging, I said, "I probably just thought it was one of those shivers most people attribute to a goose walking over their grave."

"Speaking of Aunt Pandora, Will caused her death too." I scrunched up my face in disgust. "Once he knew that the council wasn't going to fall for any of his excuses, he bragged that he had stuffed a bunch of debris into her chimney that caused the carbon monoxide to build up and kill her."

"That man was truly evil." Elissa murmured. "How did we not see it?"

"The same way the master of the dark magic hides in plain sight." Lucas had finished searing the steaks and gotten them in the oven while Elissa and I had talked. Now he took them out and slid them onto racks to rest. "These will be ready in five minutes. Can you two set the table?"

As Elissa and I took the dishes from the cabinet, the microwave beeped, signaling that the baked potatoes were done. Cole used a potholder to transfer them onto everyone's plate. I'd been worried about my cousin's food allergies, but after checking the seasoning Lucas put on the steaks and the salad dressing bottle, she'd assured me that the menu was gluten-free.

I was starving by the time we sat down to eat and immediately cut into my rib eye and forked a piece into my mouth.

Lucas watched carefully, and as I chewed, he asked, "Is it done enough for you?"

I nodded enthusiastically, and once I swallowed, I said, "It's a perfect medium."

Elissa had requested well done, but both men had chosen rare, and she glanced at their plates and made a face, "I don't know how you two can eat raw meat."

Cole winked at her and said, "Yes, you do."

Although I waited for an explanation, everyone was silent as they ate. When we had taken the edge off of our hunger, the conversation picked up, but by unspoken agreement, we kept to light topics.

By the time we finished eating and cleaning up the kitchen, I couldn't hide my yawns. Elissa, Cole, and Lucas said their goodbyes and headed out.

Lucas was the last one out the door and he lingered a second. "I'm glad you're safe now." He shrugged. "Well, as safe as The Shield can be before attaining his or her full powers."

"Thank you for your help with Will and the council." I

touched his arm. "I appreciate it."

"Seeing as you're now aware of the situation with you, me, and Pendergast, would you be willing to go out with me so we could get to know one another?"

"Give me some time, okay?" I hated seeing the crestfallen look on his face, and I hastily added, "It's not that I'm not attracted to you, I mean you're sizzling hot, I'm just a little gun-shy at the moment."

"Thank you, ma'am." He grinned, tipped his Stetson, and ambled down the front porch steps.

My face flaming, I closed the door and leaned against the wood.

Shoot! I'd have rather run naked down Main Street with a pineapple on my head than have Lucas hear the words I'd just blurted out.

Once my face stopped burning, I took a deep breath and headed to bed. I was exhausted and was sure I'd fall asleep as soon as my head hit the pillow.

Wrong!

An hour later, I was still awake, so I got out of bed and made myself a martini. My aunt had a set of gorgeous art deco glasses, and I carefully poured the mixture from the shaker into the ruby red one.

Settling into the couch, I took a sip, then cradled my glass and gazed into the contents. After a few seconds, my eyelids drooped, and when I blinked awake, I saw an image in the liquid.

It was my mother, and she was crying.

Evidently, I had just discovered how Pandora kept an eye on my mother. Now, what would I do about it?

From what I could see around her, it seemed as Mom was in a jail or a prison, but there was no way to identify the location. I somehow doubted that she'd been allowed to keep her cellphone, so I had no way to contact her.

Still, I knew one thing for sure. I had to find my mother and bring her to Echo Springs. It was the only way I could keep her safe.

It looked as if I would need to figure out a locator charm sooner rather than later.

Sighing, I headed up to the trunk to see what I could find in the Ravenscraft spellbook. Evidently, a witch's work was never done.

THE END

Thank you for reading A Call to Charms. I'm thrilled you chose to spend your time with my characters and I hope you enjoyed their story.

Reviews help other readers find the books they want to read. So before you go, please leave a review [link to Amazon or Nook], tweet, share or recommend it to your friends.

Join me on Facebook [http://www.facebook.com/DeniseSwansonAuthor] or visit my website [http://www.DeniseSwanson.com] or follow me on Twitter [DeniseSwansonAu].

Subscribe to the Denise Swanson e-newsletter for quarterly or semi-annual updates about her books and events, plus occasional recipes and other news!

Write to Denise at **ScumbleRiver@aol.com** with **Subscribe** in the Subject line and your own **E-Mail Address, First Name** and **Last Name** in the Body:

Send To:	ScumbleRiver@aol.com
Subject:	Subscribe

E-Mail Address:
First Name:
Last Name:

ABOUT THE AUTHOR

New York Times Bestseller author Denise Swanson was a practicing school psychologist for twenty-two years. A Call to Charms is the first in Denise Swanson's new Forever Charmed paranormal mystery series. She also writes the Scumble River and Chef-to-Go mysteries, and the Change of Heart and Delicious contemporary romance series.

Denise's books have been finalists for the Agatha, Mary Higgins Clark, RT Magazine's Career Achievement, and Daphne du Maurier Awards. She has won the Reviewers Choice Award and was a BookSense 76 Top Pick.

Denise Swanson lives in Illinois with her husband, classical composer David Stybr.

For more information, please check her website http://www.DeniseSwanson.com or find Denise on Facebook at http://www.facebook.com/DeniseSwansonAuthor or follow her on Twitter at DeniseSwansonAu

Made in the
USA
Columbia, SC